BAREHANDED
CASTAWAYS

FORGOTTEN CLASSICS OF PULP FICTION

For additional information about these books please visit muraniapress.com

BAREHANDED CASTAWAYS

J. ALLAN DUNN

Introduction by Arthur Sullivant Hoffman

MURANIA PRESS

Dover, New Jersey

First Edition — May 2019

Editing, arrangement and presentation of material (including Introduction) copyright © 2019 Murania Press. All rights reserved.

Book Editor & Designer: Ed Hulse.
Cover Painting: N. C. Wyeth.

Reprint History:
Originally published in the December 20, 1921 issue of *Adventure*.

ISBN 13: 978-1071107133

Murania Press, Dover NJ
For a complete list of our other publications please visit muraniapress.com.

CONTENTS

INTRODUCTION

BY ARTHUR SULLIVANT HOFFMAN

ONE DAY we in the office fell to wishing some one would do a "desert island" story about an island that wasn't a regular treasure-box of things useful for castaways; that the castaways wouldn't have a wrecked ship or well-stocked boat to draw from; that the castaways themselves wouldn't be marvels of knowledge and skill or specialists in anything that would be of great practical value on the island.

It began by our asking ourselves what kind of "desert island" story we'd like best for our own individual interest. We found that all five of us wanted the kind outlined above. The usual castaway story was all very well, but we'd read it in various versions a good many times, wanted something different, and, most of all, wanted to know what would happen to just ordinary fellows on a just ordinary island. The longer we wished, the less there was on that island and the less the castaways had and knew. We had quite an argument over whether one of them should be allowed a pocketknife and another one a watch-crystal, but finally took both these things away.

Then we decided that a lot of you readers would feel very much as we did about this kind of story. Just like us. You'd read a lot of the usual kind and probably would be as glad as we to meet some castaways that were up against it from the start, with no soft snap in the way of equipment or resources either in themselves or in the island.

We also found that none of us wanted in that story any savages: volcanoes, fierce beasts, rival parties, love element, villains, buried treasures, women or any of the rest of the exciting things that usually enter into tales of this kind. Yes, but how could a writer get any action-plot into such a story? Where would the excitement come in? Finally we figured out that maybe there didn't need to be any of that kind of excitement. Here were five ordinary, everyday fellows who were unanimous in preferring to give up that kind of excitement in the story for the sake of getting the other things we wanted. Why wouldn't there be among you readers a whole lot of other everyday fellows who would feel the same way?

So we decided to try to get such a story and find out how many of you would feel as we did. But what writer would be willing to undertake such a story, with all a writer's best and easiest material and plot-elements taken away from him? We talked our idea over for weeks and became more and more enthusiastic—kept stopping work to talk it over yet another time. But the more we talked, the more we realized how almost impossible a task we'd be handing out to some poor author.

We had all agreed that J. Allan Dunn was the man to do the story if only we could persuade him to risk putting a lot of time and work on a long story that seemed doomed to failure according to all the usual rules and regulations for magazine stories. And finally we put it up to him straight, admitting the risk and the difficulties in full. Naturally he saw them plain and hard enough without our telling him, and, not being a fool, he took time to think it over. He was interested from the first, but of course didn't want to undertake it unless he could feel reasonably sure of making good. After gathering his resources he went to it. And he found it every bit as hard as any of us had figured, but his own interest carried him along; and if the story satisfies you as fully as it does us in the office, you'll have a very good time reading it.

It was part of the arrangement that you were to be told the

circumstances in full. I also asked Mr. Dunn to state the case from his side, which he does in the following letter to you:

A. S. H. has asked me to write something of how I reacted to the plot of "Barehanded Castaways" which originated in the Adventure *office. "I'd like," he said, "to see a tale of Crusoes that would be different. Let the men be ordinary, everyday types, such a bunch of chaps as you might pick coming up from the subway. Let none of them be specialized in any craft that would be especially adapted for Crusoedom. Let there be no salvage from the wreck, no clothes to speak of, no knives, no watch-crystals to use as burning-glasses, no matches. Let the island not be one of those that extend a welcome at the very lip of the tide with convenient coconuts and self-sacrificing fish. Let them, with their everyday measures of knowledge, be up against the real thing from the start and work out their own salvation, if they can."*

He went on with other lets and hindrances. There were to be none of the ordinary adventitious aids to the adventure writer. No savages, no rescue, no volcanoes, no treasure. There was to be no attempt at a socialistic community. In fact he almost emptied out the entire box of tricks—as Jack London used to style it. He left me stranded and derelict on the keys of my typewriter.

"Moreover," said A. S. H., "in the ordinary Crusoe yarn there is always a wise man who recognizes everything that grows, crawls, swims, flies or walks and knows a thousand uses for them. Away with him!"

"Yes," I agreed, "and generally they have the fauna and flora of all the zones crammed into one little island seven by four." By this time I had got a measure of enthusiasm into me which was gradually leavening my system. "It isn't so blamed easy to get at a coconut," I demurred. "There's a heap of work, and many slips,

between sight and suction. I'd like to see you get a nut from a tall, slender, straight-stemmed palm, and I'd surely enjoy seeing you try to husk it without an ax."

"There will be no coconuts," said A. S. H. "No tropic climate and miniature Eden. No Eves. Take seven, eight or nine men. Wreck 'em. Let 'em hop to it. I'll allow you wild dogs and wild pigs for meat, excitement and leather."

Then the five of the editorial staff made up lists of what they knew that would be useful under such circumstances, what they thought they could do with their knowledge. I questioned a lot more everyday sort of chaps and I went to it.

It took me longer than any other story I have ever written. It was hard work but enjoyable. I realized how easy it is to write:

"After infinite toil he succeeded in making a serviceable knife out of a sharp stone."

"He made him a bow and arrows, practicing assiduously until he was able to bring down a bird on the wing."

"Working hard through the long, hot days, they hollowed out a log and made a navigable canoe."

And I knew how darned hard it is to do these things. Imagine yourself—you who are everyday, average chaps with average experience—turned loose in the deep woods without match or compass, knife or tobacco, with scanty clothes and no shoes. Figure how you'd make out if you were far away from all source of supplies and then multiply your troubles with a wreck, a boat voyage, lack of previous grub and water.

How to get nine average chaps ashore without a sailor, engineer, navigator or marine handyman was the first trick to turn. I knew the first forty-eight hours of their adventure would constitute the real struggle. That's where pluck and resource count. I felt sure that *all the ordinary chaps I had tackled, to say nothing of the editorial five, had not set down all that they really did know. We have got a lot of encyclopedic knowledge packed away in our convolutions that the right chain of circumstances will dredge up. Necessity is the Mother of Invention and also the Spur of Memory. That's where we have it all over the savage. He is limited by his uncultivated Imagination, still in the Stone Age.*

I had to put our Crusoes in the Stone Age. Metals of any sort are rare on such islands. Malleable metals, such as iron and copper, are non-existent. Unless I introduced a meteorite nicely blent of iron and nickel. But A. S. H. insisted on the plausibles and probables. The Polynesians, who were wonderful artificers, were Stone Age men.

So I wrecked 'em and I let them work out their plot—if it can be called a plot. I didn't try to skeletonize ahead, but tried to live with them.

It is possible to find in practically every brook two stones that will spark on contact. I've found them and made fire that way. Try it yourself some time. Ever try and open an oyster without a knife? Try to cut down a tree without an ax?

I figured that A. S. H. had in mind to bring out the hard facts of existence that are sometimes glossed a bit in romantic fiction. If he had a moral, it was that we are overspecialized, too likely to rely upon the bookshelf. Whether I have succeeded or not in writing a story that holds interest, I have tried to stick to the rules governing the suggestion. I am not pleading them as handicaps against success. To me it was interesting to realize how badly the lack of a cheap knife and especially of a saw held them back. And the psychology of it was also stimulating. I have written of things I have seen or done or heard of at first hand. May the result find favor. — J. A. D.

So there you have it. As Mr. Dunn wrote me, the main trouble was not to fall into the easy fault of just saying the castaways did a thing; which sounds easy on paper but would not be at all easy for ordinary castaways to do in real life. And, as he put it, "to make 'em human." Throughout he has done his best to make this story *real*. As to action-plot, we believe there is nothing more exciting than an elemental, barehanded struggle against nature for life itself, hour by hour and day by day, with no weapon except civilized man's brain and elemental man's courage, provided that struggle is made so real and true that an everyday human can feel it is what his own experience would be under like circumstances.

We think you will join us in thanking Mr. Dunn for having accomplished a very difficult thing—for coming under the wire a winner though carrying a heavier handicap than any other writer of a castaway island story has ever had loaded upon his shoulders. Are we right?

BAREHANDED CASTAWAYS

CHAPTER I.
THE NINE SLEEPERS.

B RETT WAS THE FIRST of the nine to awaken—or to recover consciousness. It was hard to determine his exact condition.

He felt the touch of the wind on his unshaven cheek, the grit of the beach beneath his hand. He heard the swash of the shore surf and the deeper boom of breakers on the barrier reef. He saw the sky, the color of pale amber with streaks of cirrus clouds, high up, stained purple in the sunrise—it might be the sunset. Yet these sensations barely registered. They roused in him, for the moment, no emotion. He seemed still in the thrall of the nightmare he had ridden through the horrors of the past few days that now were ending peacefully.

There had been times when he, with the rest, had acted only with the blind and desperate instinct of men in the last extremity, toys of the elements, their vitality broken down, their best efforts so helpless, the succession of incident and accident so swift that, whatever of it might have been impressed upon his subconscious memory, he could not now translate it into terms of remembrance.

He lay there weak of body and lax of will, without coordination, content to gaze at the amber skybowl, tinging slowly to apple-green, the wisps of vapor changing to a glory of crimson and orange as they sailed into the direct beams of the unseen sun. If his brain held a definite idea it was fear that behind that closed door of memory lurked terror, not only of the past but the imminent present, that the nightmare would bear him off to fresh horrors. And he could stand no more.

Little by little the tide of life within him turned from ebb to flow and, with renewed vitality, came pain. He began to ache from crown to sole. Hunger gnawed in his belly; thirst parched his throat; his body called peremptorily to his brain for relief. Above all he sensed his weakness.

The plaintive mew of a gull came sharply to his ears. He saw the beady, speculative eye of the bird turned upon him as it floated past the entrance to the shallow grotto where the nine of them had sought shelter, floored by the shingle that now began to assert its unease on his protesting back, roofed by the ledge of hard rock under which the waves had scooped out the inadequate cover.

His first attempt at movement brought nausea and dizziness. From kneeling upright he dropped to his palms until the vertigo left him, then rose and staggered a little way down the beach. The shifting pebbles bruised his naked feet and he sat down, his head ringing again, his long arms wrapped about his knees, looking half vacantly about him.

Here was a bay, a quarter-circle of water and beach, sheer black cliff that ran out into deep water on either side, perhaps half a mile between the headlands. A line of surf. Beyond, blue sea, like crinkled silk, stretching away until it blended with the horizon haze.

The sky was blue now, the cirrus clouds twists of pearly tissue. Back of the cliff the sun was shining up a new day. Purple shadow held the bay, slowly retreating shoreward. There was no sound but the rhythmic beat of the surf—the pulse of the sea—and the occasional cry of a gull, planing past, inquisitive, querulous.

The ocean stretched bright and shining, but Brett regarded it grimly. To him it looked like a monster purring in sleep with heaving sides after a wild debauch of willful cruelty and murder, licking its treacherous lips, mocking in its quietude that stored up fresh outbreak.

He was in what had once been striped pajamas of fair linen. They were still whole, though worn, but they were stained and wrinkled and all the buttons, save one, were off the jacket. Next to his skin was buckled a chamois leather money belt. In its pockets eleven hundred dollars were tucked away, three hundred in gold eagles, the rest in paper money.

Brett was tall and lean and weather burned. He had a shock of brown hair that stood up like a crest and gray eyes now sunk in deep pits that told of long continued stress. They held a light that was beginning to shine more steadily as he attained command of himself, his will, despite physical faintness, facing resolutely the phantasmagoria of despair that rose before him.

He shook in half shiver, half shudder, wrought from without and within. He felt damp and chilly in the shade. In his brain images were forming, shadowy, vague as a moving-picture film projected out of focus, reeling off the story of an ocean tragedy.

It began with the hurricane that had swept down upon them the fourth day out from San Francisco. The ocean running like rapids in a welter of white water, beaten flat, writhing under the lash, striving to avenge itself upon the ship. A lowered, sooty sky, moving on like an overhead river. Between clouds and sea, the howling and the roaring of the wind. Spindrift, driving level, thick as blizzard snow.

A phrase jumped up in his mind—like a subtitle—a phrase spoken by some one in authority—*blowing a hundred miles an hour!* But the steamer had fought it out, not without honorable scars. Some rivets had sheared, there had been too much perpetual stress of churning screws, now levering against the mad water, now spinning wildly in air. A shaft was damaged, a propeller put out of commission, something went wrong with the steering gear.

Thus handicapped they had been swept far out of their course. How far, the passengers had not been told. Brett fancied there had been no chance for observations but he knew little of navigation problems.

Repairs had been made at last and, with the weather still bad but tempering, a new course was set. There had been resolutions passed, he remembered, speeches of thanks to the captain, a subscription taken up for a presentation. Nothing for the engineer in charge.

Then, in the middle of the night, all sleeping with confidence restored, there had come the sudden shock, the canting of the vessel like a stricken beast, uprearing in agony, the grinding of torn plates along the uncharted reef! Pandemonium, the lights out! Cries and orders! The horrible, lurching slip of the steamer, the quivering stop, hung on the verge of a submarine abyss! The rush for the deck, a feeble sputter from the wireless, passengers buffeting and clawing their frantic way to the boats! Officers striving for command of the situation, the mutinous upheaval of the crew of the engine-room! Another fearful slip of the steamer! Women marshaled overside in their nightwear, hysterical, fainting.

A crowd of them—no women, thank God!—huddled in one boat as it swung slanting between the falls, sailors at the ropes in bow and stern! The slosh of the sea against the dim bulk of the partly submerged ship. Slow descent, and then——

A sickening swoop through space, the boat hanging from its stern by one snarled fall. Men tumbling with inarticulate shrieks that were swiftly silenced in the turmoil, falling into the sea like pebbles tossed out of a can! Brett, with a few others lucky enough to get fingerhold, clinging frantically to the thwarts! An upleaping wave that half lifted, half swamped them. A yell, the snarl unkinked—or cut—a confusion of the scrambling mass of men in the bottom of the boat, a furious tossing and the thrust of an oar into his hands from the stubby under-steward, Walker, taking charge in the emergency.

"Now then, shove out an oar, sir, an' 'elp pull 'er free. Git movin', you blighters—pull, blarst yer, *pull!* "

The boat moving clumsily away into the night, sloppy with water to their calves, oars out of place and time, moving like a wounded water beetle. The flare of a port-fire, the glimpse of another boat, blue and ghostly in the gleam, and, through all the mad struggle for safety, the little cockney's voice from the stern, vibrant, imperative.

"She's goin'! Look out for the suck. Pull, blarst yer, pull!"

Water that tugged at them as they strove incompetently at the oars, fighting on the verge of the great eddy that funneled to where the ship had gone down. Faint sounds of shouts across the water. Darkness! The heave of the sea and the hiss of it. The cold slaps of the gusty wind!

It was Walker, with his second-hand knowledge of boat-handling, yet greater than any of theirs, who had saved them from that first blow of Fate, leaping into the breach with the old authority he had learned in the trenches as corporal.

Later, it was Brett who had taken hold, distributing the food that had been retained in the boat's lockers during the upset, putting what cheer he could into the empty days, leavening their hopelessness.

They had four oars that had been lashed during the hurried launching, they had mast and sails. Few clothes. No compass, not even a watch between them; no better sailor aboard than the under-steward, knowing east from west by the murky sunset or a streak from the struggling sunrise. Clouds by day and night, clouds and rain and squally weather. No stars.

When the wind blew they hoisted sail and went before it, west and south. They belayed the sheet to a cleat and a gust split the canvas, snapped the rope, carried off the sail. Then they rowed at haphazard, keeping the boat's head to the seas, struggling blindly and painfully nowhere. The food down to demi-rations, scarce and sodden at that.

Haggard, despairing, helpless, driven out of a downpour of rain that ended as abruptly as a wall, the wind pursuing them. Thunder of surf ahead, the loom of land against the stars, enormous billows racing shorewards! The boat bound to a monster wave, like Mazeppa to the wild stallion. A pounding scrape, the craft filling with water, breaking up as they were borne by the shore racing breaker, grounding at last in the shallows.

A scramble through sliddery shingle and undertow—Brett helping some one whom he fancied was the professor—a last tottering effort up the slope, and collapse within the shallow cavern—the end of strength, of all resistance—oblivion!

That was the past—a dream. The present faced him—stern reality.

CHAPTER II.
A THOUSAND MILES FROM NOWHERE.

A PIECE of wood, part of the broken planking of the boat, bobbed in the shore wash and slapped on the shingle. Brett watched it idly. Finally it was left stranded. The oars, all the rest of the boat, had been back-drawn through the reef gate by the ebb tide and now drifted down the coast in a current that would carry the flotsam far out to sea.

The surrender of its plaything by the water was token that the tide was on the turn, as the stretch of shingle also showed, but Brett knew nothing of such signs, nothing of the ways of the water that he had not noticed from the deck of a steamer or as passenger in the cockpit of a launch or yacht. And not much of that. To him the bit of wreckage was merely a symbol of the greater catastrophe. The ocean had tired of its toy and flung it ashore as it had indifferently cast the nine of them.

The barren, desolate nature of the place, as its image had been registered upon the sensitive plate of Brett's mentality, began to bite in, like an etching. He roused himself with an effort, his head ringing, and got to his feet. The cliff, backed by the glory of the sunrise, appeared all the more forbidding.

It was several hundred feet high—to him it seemed as high as the Woolworth Building, and as unscalable. It rose grim from the chafing waves; it showed no terraces, no clefts up which one might clamber even a little way. There was no sign of vegetation. Not even seaweed on the monotonous mosaic of the curving beach, unmarked by rock or boulder.

Brett was thirsty, but there had been rainwater enough and to spare in the boat; he could get along without water for a few hours. But he had fasted for two days and he was faint and weak. Vaguely he thought of mussels. Shellfish were edible. But—he gazed around helplessly—where to find them?

Perhaps the tide would go out and there would be rocks with limpets clinging to them. The reminder came that he did not know what varieties were safe to eat. Many, he believed, were poisonous. Shellfish were a good deal like mushrooms and toadstools in that respect. An expert could gather a hundred varieties and enjoy them, the ignorant must leave them alone in fear.

What lay over the top of the cliff, beyond the capes? Jungle? Savages? Or ash heaps and burned-out cones? The cliff looked volcanic. Were they in the tropic or the temperate zone? Above or below the line?

Brett tried to make a calculation. It was five days trip to Honolulu. They had made four-fifths of the trip when the hurricane swooped down. Between sixteen and seventeen hundred miles southwest from San Francisco. There his knowledge began and ended. He had not bothered to find out their position the day they had started up again, after the repairs had been made. If, indeed, it had been posted where the passengers could see it. Vaguely, he fancied the gale had come from the north-east, or north-west. It would have blown them south.

They had been ten days in the boat, making progress of some sort night and day. Call it four miles an hour, four short of a hundred a day. That meant nearly a thousand miles from an unknown spot where the reefs were uncharted. *A thousand miles from nowhere!*

"My God!" The groan was half exclamation, half prayer. Brett was not accustomed to look upon himself as a religious man. He had prayed, when last he could not remember. Neither was he atheist or agnostic. The two words were the instinctive recognition of the naked will that it was face to face with the primitive, the infinite, flung purely on self-resource and rapidly realizing its stupendous ignorance and weakness. Whatever there was of egoism in the makeup of John Brett peeled from him as he looked at the placid, glittering sea, the shingled shore and the black, scowling cliff, sloughed from him as a snake sheds its skin in the Spring.

He walked painfully up the hump of the beach, where the sliding stones seemed resentfully to turn and bruise him, and looked at his comrades in misfortune.

Professor Harland lay upon his back, his veined hands on his lean stomach, one leg drawn up. The wind fluttered the scanty white hair on the fine dome of his head, his own breath lifted his untrimmed mustache with little puffings of his sunken cheeks as he breathed. White stubble gleamed like silver on his jaws. He looked very old and frail, the face already suggesting the skull, the thin wrists and legs prophesying the ultimate skeleton.

A gentle, kindly, learned man, the professor, bound on a holiday trip to a married daughter on a plantation near Hilo, wrapped up in his next edition of The Aeneid, rendered into hexameters; courteous and human, an expert at chess and bridge. He had been Brett's cabin-mate and Brett, with the whole passenger list, had formed an admiration for him that would readily have extended into friendship. The pity of this amiable gentleman's plight struck deeply into Brett's sympathy.

Next, Walker sprawled, face down on the shingle, his face on one arm. The plucky, quick-witted steward had fared better than most of them. Hardship he had been familiar with in the bloody, muddy trenches. His five-feet-four of manhood was good, tested fiber.

His face, the forehead wrinkling constantly, the blue eyes in their sandy-lashed rims always eager for what was going forward, had seldom been without a smile that showed the wide-spaced teeth. A good sort, Walker, with his snatches of marching songs and his everlasting question in the face of discomfort and danger—"Are we downhearted?"

Then Tully, clerk in the Civil Service, en route to Manila, twenty-five or so, a clean, ingenuous chap without much to show as yet in the way of development. A good deal of an infant, was how Brett mentally docketed Tully.

Bowman, asleep beside him, was a different type, slightly older. Cable operator, quick, slim, keen for his enjoyments, bewailing prohibition, dancing, flirting, inclined to play cards with richer and wiser men, hasty-tempered, self-indulgent, flying to heights of irresponsible good humor and friendliness or sliding swiftly to sullen depths of despair, railing at fate.

Of these four, the steward alone was shod and comparatively well clad in singlet, soft shirt, socks and trousers. Defter at hasty dressing than the rest, or having turned in ready for a call, Walker was wearing the only shoes in the party, a pair of canvas sneakers. The professor had on his old-fashioned nightgown tucked into a pair of striped trousers of fine weave. Tully and Bowman, like Brett, were in their pajamas.

The two next were of different mold, firemen, both of them. Oilers, rather, since the steamer had used that fuel. One was named Malone, a reckless wanderer of the Seven Seas, big boned, big framed, ravaged by intemperance along a hundred waterfronts, far from a fool, yet ignorant. The second oiler answered to the name of "Wolf."

Malone referred to him as "The Slovak." His brutish, dull face was furred with black growth of beard; his great, scooplike hands lay at the end of his long hairy arms with the horned palms up. His wide-ribbed chest labored, and he snored prodigiously. He seemed more animal than man. He had slumped under disaster, grown mutinous when the rations were shortened, relapsed into apathy for the last few days.

Brett had always been thankful he had not come away with a knife concealed about him. Like Malone, he wore a dirty undervest of cheap woolen weave and a pair of stained dungarees. Curiously, both of them had kicked off the shoes they had been wearing in the engine-room, perhaps with some dim idea of greater freedom in the water, though neither could swim a stroke.

The seventh man was a giant. He wore striped pajamas of green and white with an edging of brilliant green silk. The open jacket, the trousers tucked up to the knee, helped to reveal his magnificent body. He was on the passenger list as "Wallaby Brown." One glance at his face with its broken nose and cauliflower ear revealed his calling of pugilist.

He was returning from a not altogether successful attack upon the championships of the United States, where his brawn and gameness had been often outmatched by superior skill, though he had been a universally respected opponent. His main diversion was skylarking; he had little eyes that glinted with humor; he had been the delight of all the children aboard and his infectious laugh was unfailing.

"Well, 'ere we go," had been his contribution as the boat was swept for the reef. A laugh had backed that. That laugh was not premeditated. It effervesced in the Australian fighter like bubbles in gaseous spring water, but it had helped a lot, as his strength had often aided in critical moments. Brett was glad Wallaby Brown was along.

The last of the party was the handsomest, physically, though Brown could have broken his symmetry as a man breaks a dry stick. Even now, cheeks, chin and neck dark blue with the unshaven beard, his long black hair matted with salt-water and grit, his pajamas of actual silk—a deep purple monogrammed in crimson—the chap looked like Don Juan cast ashore. Tyrone O'Neill, he styled himself. Brett doubted his purely Irish ancestry, had been inclined to belittle his poses, his love and expectation of admiration.

O'Neill was a film star, part of a company sailing to camera the scenes of a South Sea romance upon a location that should be indisputably genuine. Brett wondered where the rest of that life-loving crowd, so curiously remote in a world of make-believe of their own, were scattered. And O'Neill, with his inordinate sense of the dramatic—and of himself as the inevitable leading man—how would he take his unchosen role in their abrupt adventure?

Sometimes he had shown signs of a different man beneath the shell. During the trip of the boat he had gloomed alone, tragic, finding, Brett suspected, certain compensations in his very discomfort. He wondered from what original walk of life O'Neill had been snatched by some smart impresario seeing in him the type to attract the girls and women who frequent the film theaters. O'Neill, spoiled, valeted, worshipped, selfish and despotic! It was going to be a bit of a shock to O'Neill when he took in their surroundings, Brett imagined, with the ghost of a smile quirking his sensitive mouth.

Brett had a sense of humor and he cultivated it. It was going to be a very valuable and necessary asset in the present situation, he figured. Unless some Golden Land of Plenty lay beyond the cliff, the nine of them were going to need all of their best qualities of courage, endurance and knowledge to carry them through—to enable them to exist.

The eight were asleep and Brett had not the heart to awaken them. While they slumbered they knew nothing of thirst or hunger or the exactions of their condition. They could do nothing to help. There was nothing that could be done except a careful examination of the cliff. If the tide fell sufficiently there might be an excursion about the capes. That should be done with caution, if possible in force.

The last word brought its own mockery as it formulated itself in thought. Aside from what strength could be expressed through their own limbs, they were helpless. Against weapons, against beasts with rending claws and teeth, they were pitifully powerless. There might well be wild animals or wild men on the island. Brett was quite convinced this was not the mainland and yet—even as he advanced to himself that assurance, it was shaken. He knew little more about it than the piece of broken plank on the shingle.

He started to walk gingerly along the beach, keeping close to the cliff because there he found the shingle regularly finer, even an occasional patch of sand, for which his feet were grateful. As he went he carefully surveyed the precipice for opportunities of scaling it.

The shadow had appreciably retreated from the sea. The two horns of their quarter-circle of imprisonment now shone in slanting sunlight that came from Brett's right as he looked seaward, a line of brightness that extended diagonally across the bay. He calculated that the beach faced generally the northwest though he was dubious whether the sun had risen directly in the east, or how long it had been above the sea horizon before it topped the cliff. In such matters he was lamentably deficient, he told himself.

Brett was by profession an editor. He was on his way to take charge of a new mid-Pacific publication that promised unusual opportunities in the light of recent interest in South Sea affairs. At heart he had ever been an adventurer. When he had first read Kipling—

Something Hidden. Go and find it.
Go and look behind the Ranges—
Something lost behind the Ranges,
Lost and waiting for you. Go!

—his blood had tingled as his heart pumped harder to the impulse of an emotion roused by the words that expressed the thoughts he had not yet crystallized, though they had often stirred the subtle chemistry of his being.

But, after school and hard-earned college, the haunting specter of Necessity, ever beside him, had stepped up and tapped him on the spiritual shoulder with the admonition that he accept the first opening. He had thought himself fortunate to find a job in accord with his taste for literature. He had tried his hand at original writing but there were others, in the beginning, who were dependent upon him. For himself he might have grinned at meager food and indifferent lodging while he wooed Success, but a dutiful son may not be a Bohemian. There were various preliminary positions, glossed with the prefixes of *sub-, associate-, assistant-*, there were certain triumphs of achievement and acknowledgment; but his success in literature was largely vicarious.

It consisted in the reading of other men's manuscripts; the judgment of them as saleable. These chaps went up and down the earth for their material and experience. Brett sorted their product for the stay-at-home reader who, with Brett, had their hours of go-fever when the mental temperature rises and ordinary tasks seem dull.

One thing amazed him now, that, out of the mass of the stuff he had edited, the tales of such castaways as he was, of adventure in the face of odds by sea and land, he had digested so little of the knowledge the various heroes had shown under predicament. Some of them had been specialized, of course—there lay the trouble. The world in general was too highly specialized. The average citizen was super-civilized, dependent on the other man's specialty, content to go to the encyclopedia.

"It's a darned shame we couldn't have brought a set of the Britannica ashore with us." He said that half aloud and laughed as he said it, reviewing his own actual knowledge of things to help them in their present strait. That didn't take long.

He knew a little very elementary woodcraft, had a slight knowledge of edible mushrooms, of ordinary carpenters' tools, of the principles of gear and lever, of bicycle machinery. He knew something of practical gardening, the groundwork of horticulture, grafting and cross-breeding. He had a small knowledge of soils and their handling. Of fishing, including drag and dip nets and the general theory of set nets and fish traps.

He understood the common principles of sailing—could handle canoes and skiffs. He fancied he could swiftly recognize coal, peat, oil indications, probably iron and copper from an unprofessional viewpoint. He could cook ordinary things well enough, except to make bread, cake, pastry. And he knew the North Star.

With the exception of the professor, he was the best-educated man of the party. He had taken the leadership, quite naturally, with full approval of the others. That meant initiative. He was in fair physical condition. His wind was good and he could outswim ninety men out of a hundred, not counting those who could not swim at all.

But how could he apply that little—that very little—list of accomplishments? His New England ancestors, striving in the wilderness, would have put him to shame. Of course the compulsion of wrestling with and overcoming immediate problems had taught them their practical knowledge of living. Nevertheless John Brett, product of the twentieth century, should have been competent to survey present circumstances with more hopefulness than he could summon.

Without tools, without hook or line or thread, without matches, even if they attained meat, found materials, how were they to provide the three essentials of existence—fire—food—water? And, beyond these three, lodging and clothing?

They would have to pool their common knowledge and apply the sum. Never were castaways more forlorn, less furnished. In all the fiction Brett had read, in the wide majority of true stories of Crusoeing, there had been something saved. Sometimes a wreck with much of value, as with the original Robinson. At the least a match or two or a watch crystal to act as burning glass. A knife. Some twine. And they had nothing.

It was beginning to get warm. If they were in the tropics, clothing might not present such a problem. But it increased his thirst. And, crowding that to insignificance, creating a distress that was almost overwhelming, the desire for tobacco wracked him. That was not to last forever but—Brett's fingers still bore the stain of many cigarettes—too many, without doubt. It had been ten days since he had seen one, and the desire gripped him fiendishly. At the moment he would have swapped a year of life for a sack of Durham and a book of brown papers.

He leaned against the cliff and looked dully out to sea. Where the sun hit the water inside the barrier reef it gave it the hue of green jade. Outside the foam-piled coral the sea was peacock blue, brazen in the tiny hollows of the swells. Gazing, Brett's heart leaped and began to pound.

He had seen a man's head! Black hair that had flared up into a sudden dazzle of reflection on its wetness and then disappeared. But a man—swimming—diving, when the owner had, perhaps, noted observance.

What did it mean?

The reflex of fright was fear. Crusoe discovering the footprint was not more alarmed. Here was a savage, spying from the water before the tribe came swooping round the cape in a canoe, yelling, brandishing clubs and spears!

Brett's will took command; his reason steadied his imagination. To the impulse of fear he opposed the determination to protect himself and his comrades. Stones were the only available weapons. He checked the shout of warning on his lips as the head broke water again, slick, shining like polished silver in the high-lights, a head retreating of forehead, large and bright of eye—a—a seal, ranging for breakfast!

There was flesh and clothing and even fuel. But how to obtain it? How to out-trick a seal in its own element without boat, without harpoon or gun? The sleek sea beast made a mock of him. It dived; it came up with a shimmering fish in its mouth.

But it had made him forget the missing cigarette. He turned again to his patrol of the cliff. Once, he fancied, it had been up-thrust from the sea, hissing and smoking, the water seething at its foot. Subsidence, or later upheaval, had provided the resting place for the beach. But, between him and the summit, there was no avenue of passage. Not even a goat could find a trail. He doubted whether there were ledges wide enough for nesting seabirds. He saw no evidence.

In the yarns he had printed in the magazines that he had edited there had always been some handy substance for the immediate preservation of life, in castaways. A coco-palm, eggs of bird or turtle, even a stranded fish, or one caught in a rock pool. The only gull he had seen still planed back and forth; no turtle would lay eggs on such a stony beach.

Surely this was the abomination of desolation. They had been rescued only for further torture. The gods were laughing. A thousand miles from nowhere—and from nothing.

The situation was invincible. Brett frowned at the word. He did not like it. Nothing was invincible except the soul of man.

There was no doubt now as to the tide going out. A rock or two began to show. There must be limpets. If he was stronger he could swim out beyond the capes. The ebb might allow him to walk around them. There must be a way in, if not a way out.

The scowling cliff gave out a sudden brightness as the sun mounted. Brett hurried to the spot hopefully. It was damp. A trickle of water ran down the trough of a shallow fluting of the formation. He touched it with his tongue. It was fresh. He lapped the rock.

He knelt and dug into the damp grit, digging with his fingers until he had scooped out a tiny basin where he watched the precious water that trailed down from some providential seam, slowly, slowly collecting. He had touched rock with his finger tips. It would not escape him altogether. It came with painful sloth. It would take an hour to get a gill of it. Six pints in twenty-four hours for nine of them! And he could not hog it. The professor was close to his limits of vitality.

Brett lay down and lapped up a little of the fluid. He filled his mouth with grit, slightly brackish yet infinitely delicious. Then he went back toward the sleepers.

CHAPTER III.
FIRE—FOOD—WATER.

BRETT AWAKENED the professor first of all and led him to the tiny water source. The scholar walked with a limping gait and the chin he tried to hold steady trembled. It was with difficulty he hoarsely managed to make himself heard through his parched and peeling lips.

"You have drunk?"

"Had plenty."

"And the rest?"

"There will be enough for all. But only about two ounces every thirty minutes. They will have to take their turns. Draw lots for it. They are asleep now."

Professor Harland seemed to have some slight scruples remaining but he knelt and sucked up the little puddle in the grit which slowly began to fill again.

"Lot of it is lost through the sides," said Brett, "but it's better than nothing. We may find some other place where the cliff leaks." Harland looked about them, pursing up his mouth.

"We'll have to do some exploring," said Brett. "Not much of a prospect in this bay. But we can get around those heads and see what we can find. No use guessing what there may or may not be. I've been figuring on shellfish from those rocks that are being uncovered. Limpets or mussels. We'll have to eat them raw. No matches."

"Umph! No fuel. That would be the main difficulty, I fancy."

Brett looked at him inquiringly.

"Figuring on a watch-glass? None in the crowd."

"No. I should imagine—of course I know very little of such matters from a practical standpoint—I should imagine the modern type of watch crystal would not be adaptable as a burning glass." He spoke with diffidence. "I was thinking of a passage in Virgil's Aeneid, in the first book. You studied the Latin classics? Perhaps you remember?"

Brett shook his head, humoring the elder man.

"It is where the fleet of Aeneas landed on the Libyan sea coast and 'The Trojans leap down from their galleys'."

The professor's tongue tripped lovingly over his syllables. It was fairly evident that he was quoting from his own translation.

"Then Achates, the crony of Aeneas, you remember *fidus* Achates, makes fire. Let me see, how does it go?

Quickly, however, Achates hath struck out a spark from a flint stone;
Now he hath caught up the fire in leaves; dry fuel around it
He hath arranged; and now he hath kindled a flame in the fagots.

"Undoubtedly Achates used steel, probably carried the whole fire-making contrivance complete, but he could have made shift with a spear-head and a stone from the beach. With some hunting he might have found two stones that, struck together, would have furnished sparks. I myself have often hunted along a brook and discovered such pebbles—kindred of the fire. Perhaps we have some steel among us—a buckle tongue? I imagine we can discover the flinty rock. This cliff might provide it. For tinder, the scraped lint of our linen. It is fuel we chiefly lack."

Brett clapped Harland lightly on the shoulder, affectionately.

"The concrete results of a classical education, properly applied," he said. "Mine didn't take. It seems idiotic not to have thought of flint and spark stones but I have been pondering over hardwood friction and remembering how almost impossible it is for a white man to accomplish it.

You've hit upon the solution. That whole cliff looks like obsidian. Good for arrowheads, too. If there is any timber on this island—if it is an is-land—we'll manage fire, thanks to the Brains of the Party. There's a bit of wood on the beach, a broken plank of the boat but it wouldn't last long enough to amount to much in the way of a fire. We'll salvage it though. There may be a nail or two in it we can make into fishhooks.

"The rest of the crowd is coming back to life. You stick around here by the spring, Mr. Harland, and take it easy. We've got to take special care of you. I begin to foresee where you will be the Moses of this company."

"It was you who brought the water out of the rock," Harland smiled. "I am afraid I shall be of little practical use. You must thank Virgil," he added deprecatingly.

Brett considered the fire-making as he went toward the seven men who were now standing or sitting up, looking toward him. He had little doubt but that they could achieve it. There were the steel buckles of his money belt with its useless contents. Some steel in the dungarees of Mal-one and Wolf. The archaic method. Simpler than the fire-drill of the Boy Scouts, over the construction of which he had been already puzzling. He reached the crowd with a degree of brisk purpose that had its effect upon them. Their eyes were dull; their attitudes apathetic. Brett had been the leader so far; they looked to him for suggestion and action.

"I've found some water," he said. "Not much. Takes thirty minutes to make a little puddle. About two mouthfuls. You can empty it in turn. I've had mine while you were asleep. So has Professor Harland. Here—"

He squatted on his haunches and selected seven pebbles from the grit, six white, one black, holding them between his palms, shaking them.

"One at a time. Man who gets the black pebble drinks first. Next to get it, second, and so on. While you're waiting for your turns, you can scout down the beach, that way, in case there's another place where fresh water comes from the cliff. Some of you can get shellfish as the tide drops. See that gull? He isn't alone. We'll likely find a colony and get eggs. Soon as we've got something in our stomachs we'll scout around those capes and find out where we're at. We're on dry land, anyway."

"I'll say it's dry," said Tully, who had drawn the seventh black pebble. "A —— of a hole, I call it!"

They did not scatter at first but gathered at the tiny waterhole. Wolf had been the luckiest in the lottery. The quantity that had collected was less than half the amount the improvised cup would hold.

"If you can wait," said Brett, "you can drink more easily and get clearer water after it fills up. It will help us to gage turns better."

The oiler looked at him with blood-shot eyes, lurching forward, his scoop-like hands extended.

"I make it bigger," he said. "That too small."

"There are others waiting, Wolf."

The Slovak stretched out one hairy, corded arm and swept Brett to one side as easily as a man might push away a child. For the first time Brett realized the oiler's strength as compared to his own. It was actually the first time that he had come into antagonistic contact with a man of Wolf's type, brawn against brawn. He had always imagined himself as being average, at least, in muscular power. He had kept up certain exercises to maintain the condition of his body. In student days he had shown strength and endurance with the best of his fellows.

But it was plain that Wolf had not exerted himself in the slightest, yet he had put him aside with no more difficulty than Brett would have set aside brushwood. Anger flamed in him. He realized his physical reaction was impotent, useless. His leadership was in peril from a man incapable of taking that position. It was a question of beasts at the waterhole. With the Slovak—might was right.

Then Wallaby Brown stepped between the oiler and the cliff, a smile on his battered face, his speech prefaced with a laugh.

" 'Old on a mo', Wolf. You're only cheating yourself. Let Brett handle it." The eyes of Wolf were as those of the brute itself. There was in them nothing of humanity, only bestial rage at this baiting of his impatient appetite. He uttered a guttural oath in his own dialect, showing his yellow teeth as he snarled and caught at the wrist of Wallaby.

The pugilist side-stepped lightly. Instead of Wolf's fingers clamping on Wallaby's arm the ten digits met in a grip that Wolf welcomed with a grin that faded instantly. Wallaby pulled the Slovak slightly toward him, swiftly thrusting his left arm back of the other's right, hand outspread on Wolf's chest, the limb rigid with tense muscles, a fulcrum against which he thrust the oiler's elbow, putting out his full strength, twisting Wolf about as the pressure became agony, threatened to break the latter's arm.

The Slovak, the pain in his eyes blent with surprise at the easy mastery of the attack, found himself facing away from the cliff and the pool. As Wallaby, still smiling, released him, Walker stood before him, cock sparrow to a crow, his eyes blazing, authority snapping from him as sparks jump from an overcharged wire.

"Back up, you blighter! There's one of you to eight of us. Put that sum on your slyte and add it up. Mr. Brett's runnin' this sheebang. You— you thick-headed, bow-legged, 'airy-skinned hape, you line up where you're told and stay put."

Wolf blinked at Walker, bewildered, like a beast that has dreamed away captivity in the night and suddenly hears the crack of a trainer's whip. He glanced at Malone but the Irishman was laughing at his discomfiture. He looked at Wallaby and Brett saw a crimson gleam in his eyes. But he knelt, swallowed the now brimming contents of the pool and shuffled off through the shingle, wading out toward the rocks that the receding tide exposed.

Bowman was next to drink. The others, satisfied as to the procedure, proceeded to examine the confines of their landing-place. O'Neill, who had drawn the third black pebble, did not go far from the pool. Wolf was thigh-deep in the water, making his way toward a weedy boulder. Walker ranged with Brett.

"Got to keep your weather eye on that Slovak," he said confidentially. "You carnt 'andle the likes of 'im with gloves. Minnit 'e starts to break loose, you got to jump 'im or 'e'll go it blind and myke trubble.

"Think we can get round those points? I don't see any beach showin' up. Looks like the rock goes down sheer into the deep water. But we bloomin' well carnt stop 'ere. Looks like a bit of a washout. Wolf's found somethink. Shellfish. Look at 'im gobbling. Crackin' the shells wiv 'is teeth. 'Ear 'im crunching."

With a display of energy that Brett could not match, the sturdy little steward went splashing through the water, up to his waist, plucking at something that clung to the rocks, searching under water.

"Mussels?" asked Brett.

"Winkles!" Walker's husky voice cleared with pleasure and excitement, as if he had been prospecting for gold and found diamonds. "Reg'lar winkle, syme as they sell at 'ome off the barrers for tuppence a pint. Pyper bag and a pin chucked in. On'y they're biled. They're a bit slimy, raw. May be nourishing but they ain't what you'd call a speedy filler. If they was whelks, now, there'd be something to them. Try your luck."

Tully had come down to join them, with Malone and Wallaby Brown. The professor sat on a ridge of sunny shingle. Bowman and O'Neill were at the pool. Brett reached a rock and began to detach the sea-snails.

"Give 'em a jerk sidewys," advised Walker. "They 'old like sixty. Want a 'ammer?" He ducked completely under and brought up a stone the size of his fist, tossing it at Brett who caught it on the fly. With it he crushed the snails on their mother rock and, picking out the broken shell, ate the viscous morsels as best he could. They were not unpalatable, but it was like feeding crumbs to an eagle to appease his hunger in such fashion.

"I want to tackle getting round one of those capes before the tide turns," he said to Walker, gulping his winkles by the palm-full, spitting out the crushed shell fragments. "There seems to be a passage between them and the reef. I'm a better swimmer than most."

"I can myke a dozen yards, dog-fashion," confessed Walker. "Better fill your belly first, if you can. You've got plenty of time. I know something about tides. Always went reg'lar for all the Summer 'olidays to Marget or S'Lennards when I was a kid, up to the time I was twenty. It's 'ighwater twice a day, twelve 'ours between tides, six to go out, six to come in, a bit later each day. It's the moon does it. Goin' out now. Enny Juggins c'ud see that."

Brett nodded. After all, the tide wouldn't make so much difference. The sea-snail diet was depressing in one way, in another it stiffened his resolution to find out what better outlook for food there might be along the coast. Birds' eggs! If he could find a gull rookery, there would be real sustenance.

"I never saw such a rotten beach," Walker went on as Bowman came down to the water. "Not even a dead starfish. No reg'lar rock-pools, no crabs running sidewise. Nuthink but these ruddy raw winkles."

"Well," said Brett suddenly, "I'm off."

"Look 'ere"—Wallaby was close to him—"what price sharks?"

Brett had thought about them, had thrust the idea from him through a mental door that he had hard work to close.

"Got to risk them," he answered with lips closing tight, his jaw set.

"Don't worry about sharks," cheered Walker. "They come in with the tide and go out with it. Syme as most of the big fish. I know that. Stands to reason, don't it? Besides, there ain't much of an entrance in that line of reef. We scraped the bottom out of the boat when the wave chucked us over it, like you'd jump a 'urdle when you're tired."

"Maybe you're right," said Wallaby Brown. "I know Sydney 'arbor's full of 'em."

Brett fancied his courage lowering as he stood there listening to the two talking about his chances with sharks. He waded out a little deeper.

" 'Ate to see you go alone," said Wallaby; "but I could never make it. Better go careful. There might be natives round the point. Cheerio!"

"Good luck to yer," called Walker. As Brett swam out with his favorite overhand stroke, he heard Wallaby's comment.

"The right sort, him." And Walker's return: "You betcher." The sun was on the water and he seemed to get some sort of vitality from it as it warmed his head, his shoulder and upflung arm. He slid along easily on the ebb, keeping out from the promontory cliff, making for the western cape. Tragedy was vanishing with action. The belief that plenty lay around the corner strengthened. The little slaps of the waves were cheery pats of promise and encouragement.

The chaps he left behind him—largely because of their inability to make the distance—were taking the matter well. They depended on him to carry them through, he felt, with a glow of responsibility. Here was adventure. Lord, he was living it!

Over the water, above the chip-chop of the ripples, he could hear the little steward singing:

A tuppenny ride on a tramcar,
Out to Victoria Park;
A thripenny ride on a roundabout
To show you're 'aving a lark.
A tuppenny shy at the cokernuts
An' ninepence for your tea;
You've tuppence left for the ride back 'ome
And there you are, you see!

"Are we downhearted? No! Look at Cap'n Webb,'arfway to the cape."

It was not all native ebullition of spirits, Brett fancied. The ex-corporal was deliberately forcing himself to do his bit to make the situation seem less serious. A good sort. And Wallaby. So far—except for the professor's helpful suggestion—it was the Britishers who had come to the front. Bowman and Tully were youngsters, and both, he knew, from inland States and towns. It would tax their best efforts to make that swim. But O'Neill? He had heard them talking about O'Neill's films on the steamer. They were of the athletic sort where the hero showed off his prowess in all lines of land and water activity. Perhaps O'Neill doubted his strength. Somehow Brett did not think him a coward.

Natation was not an acquired art with Brett. He could not remember the time when he could not swim. As the young of an animal that has never seen deep water finds itself stroking by instinct after it has been forced out of its depth into the element, so Brett swam from the beginning. Long practice and keen delight in the accomplishment had made the act as natural as that of walking.

To Brett travel by water, immersed in an element, supported buoyantly in it, not moving upright on the earth, was a translation to a higher plane of motion. He might not break speed records but it was hard to tire him when temperatures were favorable.

The barrier reef, as he had imagined, did not touch the cape. There was deep water between it and the mainland, water that ran in a swift current and a jobble of crossing waves so that he had to exert both skill and strength to get out of the pull of it.

Free from the tug, he trod water and gazed down a stretch of irregularly bitten cliff that appeared to angle sharply south between two and three miles distant, close to where an island rose from the sea, gleaming white under the sun, perhaps with guano. The cliff was of the same dark, shining rock as the one backing their landing place.

Two-thirds of the way toward the turn of the land, opposite the white-topped islet, a deep cleft showed in purple shadow. Beyond it rose a crater, wonderfully regular in formation, an almost perfect cone. Brett estimated it at about two thousand feet, realizing as he did so that he was not an expert in such calculation. It seemed composed of smooth ash or cinder with here and there a ridge of lava protruding, differentiated by shadow.

This waste slope composed only the upper half. The flank of the mountain, to his range of vision, was covered with forest, slanting obliquely down and disappearing in the rift that he hoped might form the outlet of some stream. The sight gave him fresh heart. Timber meant much. Fuel, shelter, the material for navigation, for possible escape, birds and animals living within it, good for food, to be netted and trapped.

That there might be savages hiding there, watching his progress, did not escape his thoughts. They might not have espied the group in the locked-in bay. He saw no sign of smoke, nothing but the glassy cliff of obsidian, shore-surf on a narrow beach, the shadowy entrance to the sea canyon, the island, the soaring cone of the crater—surely extinct—and the cheering green of the trees. But he decided to swim along the coast, offsetting the offshore sweep of the tide easily enough, until he was opposite the opening.

The natives, if there were any, might disclose themselves, though if they chose to come after him in a canoe he would be an easy capture. Somehow he felt convinced that the place was uninhabited. Solitude seemed to brood upon it, to emanate from it.

A flock of gulls were flying low, rising and falling. More streamed out from the island. Suddenly they concentrated, fluttering, striking, screaming over a shoal of fish. A school of blue and silver flying-fish broke water not twenty yards from him, skimming on their extended fins, sheering off at sight of him—or so he imagined.

With such a plenitude of life about they could not starve. Eggs on the island for the gathering. As for the fish, Brett began to devise traps of basketry woven from the pliant branches of trees, spread from the rocks or platforms built in the shallows from which they might spear a meal with shafts hardened and pointed by fire.

Suddenly fearful cramps attacked him, first in the stomach, rebelling against its scanty diet of water and snails. The torture doubled him up despite the desperate fight he made to resist the pain. He sank, deep, writhing, then inert. Red flashes shot through his brain, snatches of memory mingled with realization and regrets of the present issues. Pressure constricted his chest, his lungs demanded the opening of his mouth and he battled against it, conscious that defeat, annihilation was imminent.

All cerebration concentrated on one thought that appeared like a far-off light in a dark wood, growing in intensity. He must win through. They were depending on him to find them some way out of the bay where they were land and water locked. He was giving up. His will rallied to break up the apathy that possessed him. He struck out and the pain came back, now in his right leg, knotting the muscles, stripping it of power. Submerged in the warm water he broke into a cold sweat but he struggled on and up and came to the surface with his lip bitten through in his effort for control. Turning on his back, he tried to rub smooth the contorted muscles.

Swiftly as the cramp had come it left him, floating on the waves, temporarily exhausted. The gulls came and their shadows flitted over his face as they peered at him with their beady, greedy orbs and swept off with peevish cries at sight of the life shining through his eyes, though he could not have moved hand or arm against them for the moment.

A little strength came back as the sun caressed his body. He began to paddle along, slanting shoreward against the tide. Then to stroke with his legs, clipping them together. Presently he was able to turn on his side and make real progress again. At last he was off the opening of the rift. The mounting sun poured into it and he saw a vision of mauve and emerald, a glen thick set with trees marching down to narrowing water.

It gave him new impulse and before long he had passed from saltwater into fresh; he was swimming up a lagoon, a river. On one side there were glossy trees with dark red bark and curiously stilted hooping roots. He imagined these were mangroves. On the other bank, rushes. He tasted the sweet water and drank as he paddled on looking for a landing. The ravine twisted to the left, a deep gorge bristling with forest. To the right the high cone of the crater. Ahead a sandy patch of beach.

Brett was beginning to tire. The engine that furnished his energy was slowing down from lack of fuel. The snails had been an insult. They had acted like a scrap of fat thrown into a fire, doing much more harm than good.

The fresh water was less buoyant, and the current, though not swift, checked him persistently. He turned in gladly toward the sandy bit of margin that formed the corner of the stream's bank where it turned north into the deep cleft, the land rising on one hand to form the flank side, and shoulder of the crater and, on the other, he imagined, lifting to the sea cliffs. The gorge might be an eruptive cleavage, widened and deepened by erosion. As to that he did not much care, nor contribute much thought.

He landed gratefully on the sand, shoaling full length like a spent fish, lying there for a few minutes in the sun that was now well up, baking hot, drying his forlorn pajamas rapidly. It was too hot. Already he was conscious of burning wrists and neck that felt as if skinned. His cheeks smarted; his nose, as he squinted at it, was red as a lobster's claw. He was by way of being dangerously sun scorched. As a rule he tanned rather than burned, but there was a quality to this sun that was different, tropical.

It seemed to him it was more nearly in the center of the sky than he had ever noticed the sun before. He stood up and his foreshortened shadow was barely a foot in length. At the equator, he imagined, one would have no shadow at all at noon. The island was not quite on the line he thought. And the idea occurred to him that here was a way of establishing time, to mark the moment when the shadow was shortest and adopt that for noon. Between that and the same moment the next day one could manufacture a sand-clock or a water-clock divided into twenty-four—the professor would know about such antiques.

His thoughts drifted because, for the warm, contented moments, he let his mental helm swing. Suddenly it grew too hot. The tropic rays had penetrated his outer tissues and the blood in his veins seemed scalding. He looked about for shade. Rushes surrounded his sand spit, up the gorge they were neighbored by a thick clump of mangroves where some water drainage seeped and made a swampy muck of the bank. Beyond them towered tall trees.

He saw no palms and wondered at the lack of them. The trees appeared to be evergreens; the foliage reminded him of giant hemlocks. They would create shadow in their aisles and it would be cool there, if anywhere. He no longer panted from shortness of breath but it was hard, painful to breathe, as if he were in an oven.

He got up and made for the mangroves, surprised at his weakness, the uncertainty of his knees, the quick, uneven beating of his heart. He wondered if there was any shadow left back in the little bay or if they were all exposed to the blaze. Once, on a Mexican trip, he had seen two dogs shut up in a corral at noon with only a narrow strip of shade at the foot of one of the adobe walls. The wretched curs were without water and they lay gasping with protruding tongues, closed eyes and heaving sides until he had given them their chance of exit. So it would be with his comrades. O'Neill might get out of that trap—for he still believed O'Neill could swim well enough for that—but the rest of them had to stay there until he, Brett, returned to them with some sort of floating conveyance to which they could cling while they paddled around the cape and into the little river. He had thought of a raft or a primitive pontoon—two logs bound together with crosspieces.

But, unless he was lucky enough to find fallen timber and be able to launch it, how was he to accomplish that? He had no tool for chopping. A stone ax would take days of grinding to an edge, he supposed. It would have to be bound in a cleft stick—with what? With what would he fasten the cross-pieces of his pontoon?

The helplessness of it all came home to him. A Digger Indian would be more capable than he was, for all the gray matter in his cerebrum, the jumble of knowledge he would have described generally as a liberal education. It was of small use to him now in this ocean wilderness. The forest on the opposite bank seemed to regard him contemptuously, the barren cone to mock at him. It was very hot and very still; the sound of the roof was only a murmur. Vegetation was absorbing the heat, flourishing; the water was teeming with life; doubtless there were wild things of fur and feather supremely satisfied with their surroundings. He only, man, lord of all creatures, a modern specimen, was a beggar at the gate of bounty, an ignorant lackwit.

Nature was cruel. He checked that thought. Nature was as she had always been. It was man who had so changed himself by artificial surroundings that he could no longer cope with the primitive. He shut a door in that direction also. It was the law of latitudes. His race flourished well enough in its own environment, adapted to changing conditions of climate. Accident had flung him here out of his native zone where he was like a hermit crab out of its shell, without another into which to take refuge, naked, feeble, incapable of self-support. Was he not superior to such accident, the master of his fate?

"I'm going to find out pretty soon," he said aloud as he lunged sweating through the reeds, feeling his powers oozing out of him, dripping away. The first thing to do was to get away from the sun.

A sound startled him, a bird call from the woods, the notes centril-oquial, the more gibing from lack of definite location.

"You! Oh, you!" They ridiculed him stumbling through the reeds.

The mangroves stilted up from black, malodorous mud, mushy and deep. Mosquitoes sang about him viciously in little clouds, biting every inch of him, through his flimsy pajamas, stinging poison into his already inflamed exposed flesh. He was forced to make painful progress over the roots, bowed in hoops, slimy from low tide, balancing himself, clinging with both hands to the main stems. He was well committed to this progress before it occurred to him that the stream would have been his best highway. He was getting stupid with the general lowering of his vitality. He plugged on, too dull to change his mode of march.

Several times he was forced to rest, perched like an ill-fledged bird, or a sick ape, saturated with perspiration, constantly tortured by the mosquitoes. Once in the wood he could pluck a leafy branch and fan them off. The shade was only spattering and, with every motion, moisture started fresh from him until he thought the supply must soon be exhausted.

His foot scraped, was cut. He had stepped on a roughened shell. There were clusters of them on the lower rootlets of the mangroves between him and the water. Bivalves—mollusks—oysters! It was an effort for him to find the word he wanted, but, with it, there flashed up a Tantalus vision.

The restaurant at Tait's, San Francisco! Murmur of voices, subdued clink and rattle of service; an orchestra softly playing; flowers in the boxes filling the private rooms in the gallery; pretty, modish women and attentive cavaliers; scent of cigars and cigarettes; a girl dressed in Turkish fashion proffering a tray that held favorite brands—all this as a background, more or less hazy, to a cloth of white linen set with crystal and silver. In front of him, succulent oysters on the half-shell, garnished with lemon; a dish that held condiments, a glass with Tait's special sauce into which he would presently dip his oysters, tabasco in its metal-stoppered container, horseradish—he could see the little wooden paddle—!

That cleared, leaving him hanging on to a trunk with his head still buzzing, seeming light on his neck, more suggestive of a toy balloon than a head—one of the balloons they let loose among the tables at Tait's. And he had thirteen hundred dollars in his money belt! He heard himself laughing, talking aloud, listening as if it was some one else.

"The world's my oyster—and I have no sword to open it."

He was as powerless to open one of the strongly muscled cases that contained food, that meant life, as he would have been if called upon to work out the unknown combination of a vault and get at its treasure. There were no rocks between which he might crush the shells.

Out of somewhere came the derisive call of the bird.

"You! Oh, you!"

A spasm of anger shook him. To wring the cursed bird's neck!

Another memory came up out of his brain like the occasional bubbles forming in the mud beneath him.

The redwood grove of the Bohemian Club. A private camp site and supper party. There was a fire beneath an iron plate and, on the metal, oysters stewing in their own juices until they opened. Then one dug them out with a fork, blew on them to cool them, and swallowed them with gusto. *Ah!*

That was the trick! To get to the wood. To find fuel. Two stones—sparks in tinder—lint scraped from linen, the professor had suggested—then dry ferns, twigs, a fire, flat stones—the oysters atop!

It stirred him up to going on, half blinded with sweat and the cursed insects, groping, swinging, dangling from overhead boughs that gave with his weight. He knew he was talking and could not summon will to stop it. He fancied himself delirious and, with the next thought, convinced himself that this could not be, since he recognized the fact. All his body burned and throbbed with sunburn and fever. He was back in a nightmare as he had been in the boat. Yet hanging on—somewhere there was a way out!

He was walking amid great ferns, green plumes that caressed him, met above his head, were cool and springy under his sore feet, giving out sweet balm as he crushed them. High overhead a roof of boughs, springing out from columnar boles. The light was a tender green. The mosquitoes were gone, though he was automatically fanning himself with a fern frond. An enchanted wood of refreshing shadows and blessed silence—the bird no longer mocked.

In his other hand he carried a makeshift bag of his pajama top, gathered in his clutch, heavy with oysters that he had no recollection of getting. Up to his crotch he was smeared thickly with mud, now dry. From the waist up he was daubed with it, his arms coated. His flesh was blotched with red lumps. The mud seemed to act as an emollient against the stings, he regretted not having rolled in it. But he had few moments of conscious thought, his mind ran on a single track to one objective—fire. And there were no stones in this part of the forest. Down by the stream—in the stream's bed—there he would find them.

He tramped mechanically through the ferns to the hoarse strophes of an old banal jingle, repeating it with the sense that its rhythm kept him moving. . . .

Hayfoot-strawfoot-belly-full-of-bean soup. Hip!
Hayfoot-strawfoot-belly-full-of-bean soup. Hip!
Hayfoot—

A dyke of flinty lava ran down through the woods, a terrible barrier for naked feet, high and jagged. Brett followed its ancient flow and came out at the stream where it gathered in a swirling pool below a waterfall that cataracted down giant steps. The margin of the basin was strewn with rocks of all shapes, sizes and much variety. Here, if anywhere, were his sparkstones. There was a thick carpet of moss on flat boulders, and he stepped on it gratefully as he set down his oysters and drank like a hunted brute.

The moss, much of it, appeared to be kept green by the wind-blown spray from the fall. There were patches of it quite dry—dry as tinder. He collected all of this he could find and stuffed it cunningly into a funneled space between two rocks that formed a draft. Old camping experience suggested this trick.

Then he gathered dry ferns and wood. Fortune seemed to have changed her mind about him. There was fuel all about him, stranded on the shores of the stream, boughs and logs, peeled, blanched and dried, brought over the fall by freshets. One big trunk projected over the threshold of the stairway. Another lay half in, half out of the water.

First Brett tried the flinty lava, breaking off a fragment by hammering with a rock the size of his fist. Then he tested the lava on stone after stone without one resulting spark. All the time he had a feeling of being his own shadow, standing by and watching the movements of the real man as he tried, stolidly at first, then desperately, to achieve fire. The semi-madness that possessed him pumped fibrin into his muscles and gave him false strength without which he must have fallen from exhaustion.

At last, his hands bruised and bleeding, he flung from him the stone that had least seemed to offer success. It struck against one of the two rocks where he had piled his moss-tinder and pale sparks leaped and died in the sun. Brett rose to his feet with a cry that was no longer human. He found the discarded rock and pounded with it against the other. Sparks streamed under his frenzied efforts, some of them fell into the tinder, where they glowed for a moment under his breath—and perished. Brett, squatting, continued to hammer, jabbering with every blow.

"Yah-yah-yah-yah-yah-yah!"

It was useless. With a groan he hurled the stone into the pool and flung himself down at full length, played out to the limit, striving to re-member something—to collect his wits. What was it—the moss? What about the moss? It was no good. No good as tinder. That was it—*tinder*. Lint, scraped from his pajamas—scraped with what? Perhaps he could find a shell, grind it to a sharp edge, use that. There is more to the legend of the demigod who found renewed strength every time he was flung to earth than appears to the casual unthinking reader.

To a strong man of any age or race, a throw serves only as stimulus so long as he can move; a hard blow stays him, shaking his head, wary, but he comes on again boring in for victory. Brett sat up. His nostrils di-lated. Something was burning. Burning! A tiny thread of smoke went up from between the two rocks of his fireplace. A spark had persisted after he had confessed failure. It was a gift of the gods, the possession of which definitely divided man from the brute.

With trembling hands he knelt and blew gently, adding dried bits of fern, lightly as a jeweler placing weights against a jewel. He got a flare and a crackle. More fern, twigs, bits of wood, broken branches, one end of a bough. The fire leaped and roared at him as if rejoicing at birth and liberty. He dragged up more wood, tugging without feeling weight or strain. He had enough fuel now to last for hours of joyous flame.

He wanted to be prodigal with it—his own creation—brought out of stone and moss and wood, lifeless scraps combining to make this magic at his hands. He watched the smoke streaming up as if it were the banner of a conqueror.

By this time he had assured himself there were no natives, pacific or hostile. Had there been there must have been some traces of them along the stream—a trail, if nothing else. They would have no cause for secrecy. If he was wrong, this smoke, pluming black from some still resinous fragments would bring them. But he felt the risk was small.

He built up a sort of stove with one flat piece for lid, raking under it some of his plenitude of live coals, adding fresh fuel. On this lid he set out his oysters, and hunkered down, filthy, scarred, lumpy with bites, infinitely tired yet triumphant, primitive as any cave dweller. It was no petty victory to him. Much lay ahead, but he had worked out the first problem—with thanks to the professor.

One by one the shells opened and he scooped out the oysters, broiling hot, using a thorny twig to impale them, swallowed them at the risk of blistering tongue and mouth, supped the juicy residue. Never had repast tasted so delicious. Strength came back as if it were being pumped into his veins. As the blood collected for its digestive duty his head cleared. He became sane again. A little midden-heap of shells collected about him as he gorged. Languor crept over. him. Longing for a smoke now attacked him, but he was content.

Against his will his body fought and won for sleep. He woke in the ferns with a start. The bird in the woods was calling again but its note was no longer derisive. It was complimentary.

"You! Oh, you!"

The shadows had lengthened, the sun dipping toward the trees, seaward. Brett felt guilty, but consoled himself with the reflection that perhaps he had not wasted so much time. The tide had turned while he slept and he needed the ebb. Paddles were beyond him and he would have to navigate with the aid of the flow.

He went over and looked at the log that was half in and half out of the stream. It lay on shingle and he felt sure he could launch it. Before he sought another he placed the rest of his oysters on the flat, hot stone—not for himself. He did not want to return empty handed. Water he could not take. Puzzle as he might he could not contrive a container. He would have to bring them to it.

Down-stream he found another log, fairly suitable. And he picked up a pole to use as lever first, then for cross-piece. He had trouble finding the second. At last he floated the first log down to the second, beached them temporarily and went back into the forest to look for vines, taking oyster-shells as blades to hack them free. This was a tedious job against the sappy fibers but he succeeded in getting several lengths of green lianas. Wading into the water he constructed his catamaran.

It was hard work binding the cross-pieces firmly on, the lianas were none too good substitutes for rope and Brett's knowledge of knots was limited. The projections of broken boughs, helped him with the lashing and the result, though wobbly, appeared secure enough for the trip. He took along some extra branches to be utilized as a sort of seat for the professor, the rest could ride the logs and paddle with their hands. The cooked oysters he retained in their shells whose muscle-hinges no longer clamped them. He wrapped them in fern leaves and bundled the whole in his pajama coat. Finally he arranged the fire to last as long as his absence, feeding it with two big butts of boughs. With a forked stem of a young tree uprooted by some fairly recent storm, still strong and pliant for poling or fending off, Brett perched himself triumphantly upon his craft and pushed off into the current. The logs had good flotation, riding high, capable of transporting all of them. The stream caught the catamaran in friendly clutch and it went gliding along, rounding the sharp turn, making for the sea with only a perfunctory thrust or two from Brett's pole.

Once in salt water it was not so easy. There seemed to be some opening in the reef that acted as principal gateway for entrance and egress of tidal waters. The catamaran got into an eddy and drifted southward and toward the reef despite all Brett's efforts to hold it up. It sagged steadily down in the general direction of the islet, over which a cloud of gulls were wheeling against the sunset, getting ready to settle for the night.

Fatigue bound him close; his joints and muscles were stiffening now; but he slid into the water, straightened out his craft and propelled it with great clips of his legs and occasional spells of strenuous stroking, churning up the lagoon with a mighty commotion. He managed to buck the current, to cross it, to get into comparatively still water, and, finally, to find a flow that paralleled the reef in his desired direction.

Expecting to have more trouble working into the bay, Brett clambered out again on his logs. The liana lashings still held though the joints had worked loose, the structure was entire, if wobbly. And he felt as proud as the first pre-Adamite who ever crossed a river, as proud as a young skipper working his first schooner into Gloucester under the eyes of all the fleet.

Jaded in body, his spirit reacted to success. The world left behind, remote and inaccessible, with all it had meant to him, seemed for the moment well lost in the thrill of high adventure. The battling against odds, the triumph of wits left him with a sense of exhilaration that would not die down. This was life—in the raw, but vivid.

Far back, in boyish day-dreams, drifting in an old flat-bottomed boat about Silver Pond, nearby his Massachusetts birthplace, with hat over his eyes to shut out the sun, a few sunfish and perch on a withe in the bottom, and the book, *Treasure Island*, thumbed almost to rags beside him, he had, like every other boy, glorified and magnified his surroundings, transmuting them with the magic of a child's quick mentality until he had imagined himself the chief actor in exactly such a scene as this—sea girt, uncharted isle, a raft floating in the sunset, himself a Crusoe up-to-date.

Those dream-thoughts, registered subconsciously upon the records of his brain, refreshed by coincidence, rose up so strongly that Brett had the feeling that all this had happened before, or, at least, was preordained.

Faint shouts aroused him. He had cleared the cape; the bay was opening up. Two figures were at the tide edge, waving their arms and hallooing. Others joined them—five in all. One sat apart, a tiny figure of dejection, two were lying down by the cliff. The scene was sharply defined in the level rays of the sunset.

Brett had tossed chips and broken bits of wood into many a pool and watched them circle about before the main current gripped them and bore them off downstream, wandering in response to mysterious eddies whose laws he did not understand. Now, some similar vagary of the tide bore him beachward, close to the promontory cliff. He called back to those ashore, his voice cheery. Walker, Brown, Tully, Malone and Bowman waded out to meet him. The friendly eddy relinquished him; the ebb opposed. He poled hard, thrust against a rock, then found bottom, gaining distance. The five of them, armpit deep, caught at his logs as Brett joined them, shouldering the catamaran until it was just awash at the tide edge, greeting his news with eager speech of congratulation and relief.

"O'Neill's got the belly-ache from winkles," Walker volunteered. "The prof is about tuckered out. Wolf's gorn off 'is bloomin' nut. Won't have a thing to do with the rest of us. We're goin' to 'ave trouble with that blighter. Wot's in the parcel?"

O'Neill was evidently sick in soul and body. He had vomited until he was limp; his face was gray-green; the ends of his fingers wrinkled. But the news of fire and water and food provided revived him to an effort. He had grit in him, Brett decided.

The professor was wan with the long fight of his spent forces of a sixty-five-year-old body. But he had a smile on his lips and in his eyes and essayed a show of vigor. The cold, cooked oysters were shared by all except O'Neill, a skimpy ration for each, yet it fired them up a little. Malone took Wolf's share to him.

The oiler paid no attention to Malone as the latter argued with him, pointing to the catamaran, finally leaving him in disgust. But he thrust the food into his mouth and, as the rest gathered round their craft, came down the beach and took his place with the others, four astride each log, the professor on a precarious platform made from the extra boughs.

Brett set the stroke, seated ahead on the right-hand log. They all began to scoop with both hands in unison. The catamaran commenced to move along smoothly toward the cape. Inside the reef it was smooth water and they made good progress. The sun sank but it was still warm, the water the temperature of new milk. The sky was clear and brilliant stars came out, reflected in the lagoon.

A moon sailed up over the crater as they made the mouth of the stream, and, stimulated by the sight of the trees, the closing presence of their destination, they drove their way up the little river. Like Brett, they presently lapped the fresh water and that supplied nervous energy for the finish of the trip, halting once, paddling ashore to gather oysters.

When they saw the glow of the fire, burning cheerily, its smoke column tinged crimson, waving in the wind that funneled up the gorge from the sea, all hands, save Wolf, gave a cheer, hearty enough, even the professor lending his voice, and O'Neill, who had been shivering for the last half-hour, keenest of all of them.

They were all badly sunburned by their exposure. As Brett had feared, since noon the beach had held no shade. They had tried relief by sitting in the water but the radiant heat from its surface had begun to actually crisp their faces and they had found the greatest relief from sand burial. O'Neill's skin, from his outdoor posing, had stood it better than any, but he had suffered severely from the touch of ptomaine that had not affected the rest, except for Brett's cramp.

They were not very talkative. They accepted the fire and the oysters as gifts for which they were duly grateful but showed it in actions rather than with words. The wind that had started at sunset steadily increased and sang through the boughs of the great trees in mimicry of the breakers whose booming it out-noised.

Bowman, Tully, Malone and Brown gathered driftwood and they piled the fire, both for comfort and for fear of losing it, though Brett felt sure he could repeat his sparking feat more readily a second time. They would not let him move a finger. Wolf sat close to the flames, unmoving, his eyes, when they turned toward his fellows, without animation, reflecting glassily the red of the glow that played over his hairy arms and legs and swart, short-bearded face, making him look like a Caliban.

O'Neill lay back to a rock on a bed of ferns, reveling in the heat, slowly recovering. He had managed the hot oysters without nausea. They had all come fairly well through the first day, Brett considered, sleepily, and better times were ahead. Tomorrow they would make fish-traps, secure eggs from the bird island. Today they had attained the three prime necessities—fire, food, and water—sufficient for their sustenance.

CHAPTER IV.
THE POOL OF KNOWLEDGE.

PHYSICAL EXHAUSTION, filled stomachs, comparative ease of mind, coordinated for slumber, and the nine slept soundly through the beginning of the night, despite their sunburned flesh and the stings of occasional mosquitoes. They all lay to leeward of the fire and what smudge it made. The insects were not numerous above the mangrove belts and the wind that drew steadily up the canyon kept them scattered. Stacks of the great ferns made luxurious fragrant beds, even for restless people. The night was warm and balmy.

Brett awoke, looking straight up to the moon, high in the heavens, his body tingling, his emotion centering in alarm. Of what, he did not comprehend. Not a sixth sense, but certain of his natural sentinels, had registered an automatic call that summoned Consciousness. There is no such thing as a sixth sense.

The sensatory nerves of some men are more acute than others by inheritance, training, experience. There is a closer connection between their conscious and subconscious minds. Those who live amid peril, know peril registered in waking moments, whether that danger be constant or transitory, become what is unscientifically known as keyed-up. There is no such thing as tautened nerves. Physiologically such a condition is impossible. They are not thread but a chain of close-lying neurons that may be stimulated into linking up and the conveyance of a message, like the nickel filings of a wireless coherer. They may be synchronized, the ganglia stations made more alert by the mental stimulus of caution or of fear that causes energizing secretions to flow from the glands whose utilities science is just beginning to understand.

Of the nine, eight awakened at the same instant, thrilled by a sense of danger. Wolf alone slept on. He had the least ability for control of all of them, the least education, the least imagination. The perils of the boat voyage had rendered his mind torpid, his reasoning almost nil, had slowed down his system. Brett heard Wolf snoring, as he looked and listened, conscious of stirrings from the others, sure they were awake.

Out of the woods across the river there sounded a fearful cry. It was a deep-chested, savage roar—or coughing bay—indescribably vicious. Out of the forest back of them that rose to the cliffs, there came an answer, a hideous, prolonged howl that ululated through the night with a menace bringing the eight of them simultaneously to a sitting posture.

A tremor traversed the marrow of Brett's spine, his skin goose-fleshed and, for the first time in his life, he experienced the weird lifting of hair, not only on his scalp but a feel of ghost hairs bristling where none grew. He had edited descriptions of such phenomena, accepting them as one of the tricks of adventure-fiction writers. Now he knew the fact. His throat parched; sweat broke out before his will reacted, marshaling force to fight off panic. The wind had died down to infrequent whisperings.

"Mother of God!" he heard Malone whisper, next to him, saw the big Irishman cross himself. "Mother of God, 'tis a banshee!"

It came again, the guttural, sonorous roar beyond the river, the hideous howl from behind them. Brett's imagination conjured up a picture of a jaguar, slinking through forest glades, calling to his mate that the quarry was found, that it lay between them, bidding her join in the stalk. He could visualize big cats stealing down, nostrils snuffing, eyes lambent, eager for prey.

Silence—pregnant with dread. He saw the eyes of his comrades, wide open, staring, mirroring the light of the fire, their faces ruddied, their body outlines silvered by the moon. Fire—that was their weapon. Brett rose, found wood, tossed it on the coals, threw on some dry fern that crackled as it leaped into a gush of flame and revealed them plainly to one another. He picked up a flaring brand and stood waiting, expectant of leaping brutes. Wallaby Brown and Walker followed his example, O'Neill and Tully snatched burning clubs from the fire. Bowman seemed held in a paralysis of fear. The professor showed no signs of panic though he did not rise, and Wolf snored on.

The fire pulsed, painting rock surfaces, fern fronds, the distant trunks of trees and the tangle of shrubbery that encircled their little camp. The constantly shifting highlights emphasized the shadows out of which attack might come from any quarter. The moonlight, filtering down, caused great patches of mysterious gloom with pools of tremulous radiance.

Sudden awakening in the hour when the furnaces of the body are banked, life at its ebb, helped to emphasize the feeling of a hidden horror that licked hideous lips in ghoulish anticipation, knowing its victims were battling with fear and uncertainty. The moments were packed with dread. Dread crept in upon them through their sight, baffled and distorted by the night; through their ears, listening to strange sounds, unable to place their direction; through their imaginations that conjured up all they had ever stored of jungle lore.

It plucked at their will, strove to unravel the weft of reasoning that urged them to stay firm. Panic slowly rose about them in that awful silence, as the tide rises, inevitable, overwhelming.

"Tchk!"

It was O'Neill who made the sound, with his tongue against his teeth. His head was turned so that he looked over his right shoulder toward an arm of the forest that ended in spatulate masses of undergrowth reaching to the shelving bank of the little river. Between two of these clumps, gliding swiftly, too fast for definite impression, Brett saw a beast passing with motion that suggested both grace and strength. At the sound of O'Neill's cluck it paused for a moment and its eyes showed like two small lamps, powerfully phosphorescent, green, cruel and menacing.

Then, noiselessly, the creature moved on, invisible against the background of the next copse. It seemed as large as a calf but of far greater symmetry. It was followed by a second—a third—a fourth, each padding fast and silent across the open, halting for the infinitesimal space when their orbs glowed green, turning toward the fire and the men who stood ready with their impromptu, inadequate weapons; dissolving into the blackness and at last, entering the water unseen and swimming rapidly across a pool lit by a wide bar of moonshine showing great heads and prick ears, fanlike wakes, landing in dense shadow.

They had come and gone so swiftly that Brett wondered whether they were not phantasms of his own imagination, forgetting that O'Neill had seen them first. Now Walker spoke in a strained whisper.

"W'otever they were they ain't after us. And that 'elps some. Mebbe the fire scared 'em off us but looked to me like they were on to their original job. W'ot did you figger 'em for? Lions?"

"There wouldn't likely be lions on an island," suggested Tully. "Lions wouldn't take to water that way, would they?"

"I don't know about that," Brett answered. "But we don't know this is an island, Tully. It may be the mainland! We've got to go exploring before we find out. To the top of that cone. I think—"

Across the river pandemonium broke loose, as if the arrival of the four beasts had been the signal for the release of a devilish pack that now gave tongue as they raced ravening through the forest reechoing with their howls. Either they had scented or sighted their quarry or they despised them, giving reckless tongue that might perhaps affright their prey, rob them of speed.

The chase swept on; its hubbub died down; broke out afresh. With it there seemed to blend deep-chested grunts of defiance, then a shrill squeal or two of terror. The night was filled with the noise of brutal combat, snarls and howls and roars that suddenly subsided, died as completely as if the earth had opened and the fiendish band taken a short cut back to hell with their victims.

That was the end of sleep. The uproar had wakened Wolf and the savage clamor seemed to have stirred in him some beastly affinity. He stood with his head thrust forward, listening eagerly, with glittering eyes, like a big ape in sympathy with the hunting of his comrades of the wild.

Then he squatted down on his haunches and remained in that position until the dawn broke.

Brett fought back Fear that closed in around him with steady pressure, attacking mind and body. The great ally of Reason, Experience, was lacking. All that he had read, had heard, tended to make him regard himself as the most defenseless of living things. Man, armed neither with talons nor efficient teeth, tender of skin, vulnerable. He seemed like a being out of its element. Every time he remembered the agile brutes crossing the stream, he shuddered and such perverse remembrance perpetually asserted itself despite all the efforts of his will to dismiss it.

One thing they had—most necessary—fire. They must contrive some sort of clothes to shelter them from the sun, shoes to protect their feet, hats to guard against the heat, some kind of dwelling where they would not have to repeat this dreadful night and could feel secure from the beasts that might take it into their mind to hunt them. Weapons, too, must be invented. In the night the odds seemed stacked against them, the land unfriendly.

The cone of the extinct volcano rose naked from its mantle of dark wood. It glistered like frosted silver under the moon and stars. The wind began to gather force again, breaking in gusts, as if great bubbles formed and burst in the blackness, the rush of it stroking through the tree tops with the long swish of the backwash of waves on shingly shores. In the intervals the reef surf boomed softly. Wind and surf emphasized the silence of the night after the frenzied clamor of the pack.

The fire crackled, shifted, ashes shuffled, but all these things were elemental, vast, a part of Time itself. To them the fate of men meant no more than the panic of ants in their underground council hall when the foot of a giant treads on their hill.

The burnished stars, the bright moon, the naked lava of the cone, the wind blowing through the vault, the vexed sigh of the trees—the stark lonesomeness of it all, permeated him. His will retreated, his ego shrank.

Pin pricks on the scroll of eternity. Motes floating in the light. Shut off from even their own little world, marooned, encompassed by danger, huddled under the light of stars whose beams had taken a million years to penetrate the regions of the air, a million years to project a speck of golden flame that might be the ghost of a world long since dead of flame, even vanished from the firmament.

To follow such unsatisfactory thought was to commit mental suicide by plunging into the gulf of infinity. Brett roused himself to physical action, mended the fire. The rest were wide awake and he started low-toned conversation.

Wolf remained, squatting. He was not far from the brute. Accustomed to heavy toil, constant command, a slave by inheritance, the Slovak was short of imagination, knew no necessity for emotional control and was the servant of his senses. If Wallaby Brown had the limited mentality of a boy, Wolf's equipment was that of a dull child of half his age. What should have gone to brain had over-developed brawn.

He might have grappled with one of the night-hunting pack, Brett fancied, meeting their ferocity with a glad lust of combat and joy in the power of his muscles. Brown alone might match his strength—none of the rest of them. Wolf was the type, thought Brett, that in such savage surroundings, would rapidly lose his humanity, revert utterly, willingly, to animalism. He might even become dangerous to the rest of them unless he was watched and handled. Malone had the most influence over him and Malone, wild, undisciplined descendant of rough Celtic kerns, was none too easy of management or restraint.

Management was needed, Brett was certain. They must combine together, pool their knowledge, their efforts, use to the best advantage their especial gifts. Exploration might determine them to be stranded on the coast line of a continent, but he felt intuitively that they were on an island, uncharted, far from the lanes of ship travel—doomed to live there for an indefinite period, perhaps for the rest of their lives—for how could they hope to get away? He faced this as a fact though he did not think it wise to try to carry the talk beyond present emergencies.

"There are two main things to be done tomorrow, it seems to me," said Brett. "One is to get some nourishing food and the next to find a cave where we can sleep securely. We are down to primitive conditions, for the present. Cavemen's conditions and lacking cavemen's endurance. Back in the stone age. We'll have to manage with stone axes, spearheads and other weapons in case we are attacked by the animals. We may even be attacked by savages.

"Those can neither be found nor manufactured in a day. A cave where we can pile up stones across the entrance, with a fire, smaller stones to throw, bigger ones to roll, seems to me the most feasible. We can make lean-tos, fern-thatch shelters, later on, but you remember the rain we came through before we sighted the place. There is a heavy rainfall here, to my mind—though I am no woodsman—by the look of the trees and the ferns. These logs have been washed out above the falls by the stream swollen in a storm. This may be the rainy season; it may rain off-and-on all the year round. We've got to be prepared for bad weather, both wet and cold."

"I've 'eard 'em say that some of the bloomin' South Sea natives build what they call treehouses," suggested Walker. " 'Ow about that? I know the Filipinos build on long piles."

"If we could find the right group of trees we might manage some sort of platform," Brett answered dubiously. "I fancy they use bamboos a good deal in South Sea building. It wouldn't be an easy job for us to cut down a bamboo or any other tree for that matter. A cave first, I think, and that's your job, Walker. You are the only one can do much walking."

"I'll give the loan of my sneakers to ennyone who wants to go cave 'unting," said the steward. "That menaggery we 'eard breakin' loose 'as got my number. I don't believe I funk easier than the next cine but it ain't goin' to be a picnic roaming through the woods, thinking every minute one of those beauties we saw swimming the river is trailin' you, licking its bloody chops whenever it thinks of your ribs. My flesh ain't stopped crawlin' yet."

Brett nodded. He had an idea—a hope—that the beasts might be nocturnal in their habits—that they might turn out to be afraid of man—either as a known or unknown quantity. But he appreciated Walker's frank exposition of his feelings.

"We'll fix up some sort of sandals," he said. "Perhaps of bark. Or we may see a cave from the stream. My idea was to try and catch some fish tomorrow and to paddle our craft out to that island for birds' eggs. There may be berries or fruit of some kind. We could divide into two or three parties. Walker's right. None of us ought to go about alone until we know more about the habits of those beasts."

"Wish I had a chunk of whatever they were hunting," said Malone. "I'm tellin' you meat 'ud taste fine to me. The oysters was good, but my stummick's forgotten it ever met them. How the blazes are ye goin' to git fish without string for a line or to make nets with, lave alone hooks? Chase 'em up on land or swim after 'em an' scoop 'em out?"

"We might make a dam in the river," suggested Tully. "Just above a pool, so the water would run out and leave them in the shallows."

"Sure," said Malone sarcastically, "it's easy to build a dam. You do that, my son, an' Bowman an' me'll go bird huntin'. We'll find some salt an' I'll whistle 'em down so's Bowman can put it on their tails. Mebbe there's crawfish in the river an', if you go wadin' long enough, they'll nip your toes an' you can walk ashore with your supper."

"Tully's idea might work above the falls where the pools would be smaller. If there are any fish up there. The trouble is we are none of us qualified for a trip like this."

"It is singular," put in the professor in his mild voice, following Brett's lead, "how dependent we moderns are upon specialized manufactures. We are so accustomed to going to this man or that for the simplest articles that when we are thrown upon our own resources we are comparatively helpless. Take myself, for example. I could never manufacture anything. It is a difficult task for me to drive a nail with any ease or accuracy. As to supplying the nail or the hammer, I should be utterly lost.

"Yet our immediate ancestors—mine, at least—building themselves houses in New England, supplying agricultural implements, found iron ore, smelted it, made their own straps and hinges, their bolts and nails of the hammered metal, wove their own wool for clothing, hewed their own lumber, sawed their planks, built their houses, ground their grain, made bricks, provided for themselves entirely in an inclement climate. Every man was more or less an artisan."

"They had axes and saws, guns and ammunition, a heap of things they brought over with them," said Bowman. "We haven't even got a worn out jack-knife. One good ax, a rifle and a few shells would go a long way toward making us comfortable. We're right up against it, I'd say."

"There might be iron ore round here," Tully put in.

"Would you know it if you saw it?" Bowman demanded.

"I think so."

"How are you going to smelt it?"

"I don't know that. I suppose you could build some sort of a furnace with layers of charcoal and ore, and drafts to keep it red hot. The metal would flow off, I suppose."

"Huh!" Bowman snorted contemptuously. "And then what? What are you going to make of it, all mixed up with charcoal? How about the slag? How about your molds and your patterns?"

"Know any more about it than I do?" retorted Tully.

"No, I don't."

Brett lessened the growing tension. "First catch your iron or other metal and then start experimentation. We're still in the Stone Age. If we advance to the Bronze we ought to be able to do as well as the races who first made that metal. The Greeks, professor?"

"Or the Phoenicians. The shield of Achilles, according to Homer's description in the Iliad, was made by Hephrestus throwing into his furnace copper, tin, silver and gold. Copper and tin formed the earliest alloy, as I remember. Up to four hundred B. C. Then they used lead. But I know nothing of the process—nothing. I find myself a very ignorant old man in these circumstances. Left to myself, I do not think I should be alive very long. I lack both strength and wisdom.

"The ancients stored their knowledge in their brains and taught it carefully by word of mouth and by example. The art of writing has advanced man wonderfully but it has reduced the personal factor of his efficiency. We are too used to go to the bookshelf for our information, as we go to the stores for our physical needs, to depend upon the specialist for anything else except the thing we ourselves manufacture.

"I am a worker in words. Words are not useful for preserving life. I doubt if I could catch a fish. I never have done so. I know nothing of cleaning it, I should probably spoil it in trying to cook it. I could pick berries—but I would not know if they were poisonous unless they were familiar species. I can hardly be counted as one of the helpful members of this party," he ended, with the first touch of bitterness in his voice that Brett had ever heard.

"I am a dealer in words also, professor—or was—" Brett said. "I have gone over my own capacities and find I measure up with yourself."

"That be blowed," put in Walker. "You—you've got more guts than the lot of us. You go ahead and *do* things. We'd be on that beach yet if it 'adn't been for you, and we'd never 'ave reached it if it 'adn't been for you. I've been in the museums and seen wax models of cavemen large as life and twice as natural—a hugly lot without hany plyce above the heyebrows for brains. They got by—didn't they? An' we've got brains if we use 'em. Got a lot of stuff packed away there if we can dig it up. Necessity is the Muvver of Hinvention. I used to write that on my slate w'en I was a nipper. We've got brains and it's quality what counts, at that."

"You're talkin' fine. Now go ahead and invent somethin' by way of example."

Walker scowled at the mocking Malone. "I'll match my wits aga'nst yours, my bucko!"

"Let's all tackle the prime problems first," said Brett. "Some of us have lived out of doors, more or less. We've camped maybe, or have been brought up in the country. If we try to remember all we know about fishing and hunting and setting traps we may be able to put the practical things into practice. You know what I mean—woodcraft as applied to getting food. Later, for providing clothes.

"There was a man went up into the Maine woods one time on a bet that he could go in naked and stay there a month. He, or another man, did the same thing in California. There were suggestions that they did not live up to all agreements, but that is the sort of thing I am driving at. I imagine we'll all feel less worried about the animals when daylight comes—I know I shall. Unless you chaps want to sleep, why not put in the time figuring out our united knowledge and how to apply it? How about you, O'Neill?"

"Me?" The actor shrugged his shoulders, the firelight showing his handsome features drawn to a sulky cast as he shifted his position. "I don't know anything about the Daniel Boone stuff. I'm bothering my head how we're going to get *off* this infernal place rather than planning how to make ourselves comfortable for the next year or so."

"That ain't 'arf a bad idea," said Walker, sarcastically. "Got any suggestions, O'Neill?"

"My name's Mr. O'Neill to you, Walker. You're forgetting your place."

"Don't you ever think it. Never 'ave and never will. I've paid out my money to see you doin' your stunts as the bloody 'ero on the screen, but b'limy, you ain't no ruddy 'ero in this show. All that plyce stuff was left on the steamer, went down with 'er, got washed off in the boat. I'm a blasted aristocrat along of you. W'y? Because I've got a pair of shoes, for one thing." He shoved the sneakers aggressively into the light.

"You think you're the only one who's got a 'ome and wants to git back to it. Though it ain't 'ome you're after. It's the bright lights and the big salary, the mash notes and the fool girls saying 'Ain't 'e grand?' You myke me fair sick and you 'ave right along. Always 'ad things cut and dried, you 'ave. Now you'll ruddy well sweat for w'ot you get like the rest of us."

"No sense in quarreling, Walker," said Brett. "All our nerves are on edge. You didn't give O'Neill a chance to finish."

"I'll apologize for what I said, Walker. I'm wound a bit tight. And a lot of what you said is right. I'm not much good off the screen. I've always had property men walking round handing me the goods. It's a bit funny when you think I starred in *Beneath the Southern Cross*. Just such an island as this it was supposed to be. And I was the man who came into camp with the food, killed the beasts, fought the savages, and generally saved the situation.

"It went so big we started to find a real location for a similar picture. The first was largely faked, as to scenery. If we ever get back I'll be able to write the continuity of a true-to-life scenario. But I was born back east in a city and I've always lived in a city—when I wasn't out on location— and I drove to that and back in my own car. I never fired a thing but a blank cartridge and I've never caught or killed anything bigger than a mouse—don't know as I've even done that. I've been a trapper and a hunter, a lumberman, a castaway, a cowpuncher, a sportsman—on the screen. I've got all the costumes and I've gone through all the motions but I've never tried to even cook an egg.

"I'm fairly sure I know the North Star but I don't know the Southern Cross. Before I went into the films—Walker's right. He's a bigger man than I am, and a better, if only from the standpoint of wardrobe. If you ever get any dishes you can give me the job of keeping 'em clean, Brett. I might be able to do that. I—Oh, my God!—" he ended abruptly, his face working with the anguish of self pity as he got up and walked to lean against one of the near rocks on the flat top of which he set his folded arms, burying his face in them, his shoulders shaking with emotion.

"Always in the pose," said Walker, *sotto voce,* but there was no spite in his voice. O'Neill's apology had cleared the air. Brett fathomed the poignant distress of the ex-star, pampered during every waking moment, suddenly shut off from a life filled with what O'Neill considered success. There might be something more than self-conceit back of that break-down. He wondered what home ties might lie behind Walker's remark. Suddenly his fellows in misfortune grew more important, more tragic.

Brett himself had left friends behind, no near relatives. There had been a woman once but the curtain had long ago rung down on that episode. Professor Harland had his married daughter, happily provided for, free from the parent stem, creating her own world, already regarding her father as likely to pass out of her life before it had reached its own maturity. Harland's wife, he believed, was dead, and there were no other children.

But the rest? Bowman played butterfly with the girls aboard ship, but there might be a family he loved, by whom he was loved. Tully the same. Tully might well have a sweetheart; there might be a touch of real romance there. Wallaby Brown, prizefighter as he was, was the type who might well have a wife and kiddies—he was such a big good-natured boy to youngsters—waiting for him in Australia, and Wallaby would make a good husband as well as father.

Malone—no, not Malone. He was only a drifter. All his wages went into his belly and to pander to his coarse desires. Still—even Malone and Wolf might have women and children dependent on them.

So far the course of events had moved too swiftly, the termination been too abrupt, the present situation too fraught with uncertainties for such reflections. To be out of the world, out of the hurly-burly, out of the struggle and the shams on a place like this held no terror, no pain of severance for Brett. He supposed he was a bit of a cynic, a bit of a hermit. He had often told himself he was sick of sitting up to the veneer and wanted to put his legs under the cruder table of a more red-blooded life.

He was doing it now with a vengeance. Life reduced to a contest—not against his fellow man, but against natural forces—for food and clothing, warmth and shelter, and safety from the beasts that were stronger than he was but were beneath him, knowing no reason.

The contest appealed to him. It roused up primal, atavistic impulses long since buried under civilization but handed down from generation to generation. From the moment he had awakened on the island he had taken up the challenge of the wild with a zest that, looking back, he now appreciated had accompanied all his toil. But with the rest it might be different. He switched off the current of his thoughts and listened to Bowman, now talking.

"I was born in the hills of Vermont—" There was a trembling catch in the youngster's voice that he forced out of it bravely. "I got some superficial knowledge of woodcraft. That is, I know North American edible plants. I can build a fire—if I've got matches. I used to think I was a wizard because I knew enough to strip the inside bark of birch in wet weather to start the blaze. I've built a shack—with tools. I'm a rotten fisherman—never could catch them when the other fellows had a string. I never did any hunting.

"Once I built a canvas canoe that was navigable. Built it from plans and it wasn't a bad job. But I had all the tools and materials again. I worked on farms—our own and others, for two or three Summers, but it was only unskilled. work. I couldn't plow, I had no knack with horses. I milked, picked fruit and pitched hay, weeded.

"I've read a lot of Dan Beard's books and I must have a lot of odd facts stored away that'll maybe crop out later, but even Dan Beard presupposes tools to work with.

"What else? I read a heap of scientific books when I was a kid—more scraps of knowledge there. Monkeyed with electricity—batteries—wireless later on. Took chemistry in college. Did well in physics and mathematics—and there isn't a thing that helps now. Not a thing!"

"I don't know," said Brett. "Those odds and ends of yours will meet many an occasion, I expect." Bowman laughed.

"I might be handy round a bungalow. In the wilderness I'm a joke."

"No bigger joke than I am," said Tully, seated next to Bowman. "The only thing I am an expert at is driving a Ford." The statement got a laugh from everyone but Wolf. Tully went on with his list of accomplishments pertinent to the occasion. It was much like that of Bowman. He added that he was well grounded on Army principles of sanitation with first-aid knowledge of medicine and surgery gained in the war.

"I think I could make a clam-shell knife, or from some other shell. You can sharpen the edge on a rock. I've cleaned fish that way, back East. My idea of a weapon is the right kind of stone bound in a notched branch. Rawhide would be best for the binding. It would shrink as it dried. At least I suppose it would. I've always read so.

"If we could find a runway of some of those brutes that were howling tonight, dig a pit there, cover it over with twigs and then dirt, drive sharp stakes in the bottom, we might get one of them. We could finish it with stones or with a hardwood spear. Then we'd get the hide for strips to make into lines and nets and for weapons. We'd get the sinews to make bows and we might be able to eat the flesh. If we got more of them we could scrape the skins, salt them, soften them with brains, use them for shoe-packs, for clothing. Scrape 'em with shells, stretch 'em."

"Sounds fine," said Walker. "We're getting along first rate. Only—"

"Sounds like Fenimore Cooper," said Bowman.

"It could all be done," retorted Tully hotly. "What if I did get it out of books?"

"It might be done," said Walker, "if you could dig that pit. What was you going to do it with? Clamshells? Or your fingers?"

"Well, what have you got to offer us that's better?" Walker grinned.

"Me? Not much. I was born in 'Oundsditch, London. But my old man knew a bit about trappin'. He was w'ot they call a poacher. He came from Surrey. 'Olidays he'd take me with him, out to 'Endon, or to Tring Ressyvoy, maybe to the River Lea above Chingford and he'd teach me all 'e knew. Trigger snares for rabbits. 'Orse'air loops and lines. Many a partridge I've copped, and snaked basking trout and pike with a lassoo back of their gills. 'Ow to get frogs and eels. But what's the use? No 'orse'air; no 'ook. W'en I was a nipper I've caught sticklebacks with a bent pin. Sticklebacks and minners. You 'ad to sling 'em out quick 'count of there being no barb. Maybe we could make some sort of a 'ook out of the nails in that bit of a boat. Winkles for bait, or oysters. O'Neill and Brown 'ave got the line right in their silk pajama cords. I might fix up a snare or two. But we don't know what kind of animals there are round 'ere. Don't know their 'abits.

"My guv'nor used to make baskets. Bit of a gipsy, 'e was. I've watched 'im often enough to tackle a weaving job. If I can find some sort of withes or willers, I might make an eel-pot or two. Make some for crabs. Bait 'em with shellfish, weight 'em down with rocks, set 'em where you can get 'em at low tide.

" 'E used to lime birds. Make the birdlime out of 'olly bark. Smeared it on twigs. Wouldn't wonder but what we might find some sort of sticky stuff 'ere. Showed me 'ow to cook 'edge'ogs in clay. None of them about, likely, but fish is prime the same way. That's all I can think of now."

"You get the prize, so far," said Wallaby Brown. "I've killed rabbits by shying sticks at 'em. Might do it again. If there's any rabbits. I've fished a bit and I can cook beach-fashion. Leastways I know how it's done. Dig a pit in the sand—that ain't hard work—line it with stones—start a good fire in it and let it burn down to charcoal. Wrap your grub in leaves—or seaweed—put it in and cover up with more green stuff. Pile the sand on top and leave it overnight. I've seen fish and chickens cooked like that and they tasted prime. Sucking pig, too. Only that took two days. Kanaka style. Natives off the trading vessels introduced it to Sydney and now all the beach parties cook that way."

"Like a clambake," said Tully. "Clams and lobsters, chickens and sweet potatoes all steamed under the seaweed. Oh Lord!"

"Me too," cried Bowman. "I vote we talk about something else than eating. This is worse than nightmare."

"There's Malone to hear from yet." This from Walker, not without certain malice to tease Bowman. Brett smiled to himself. This talk in the last quarter of the night had been a good thing. It had diluted the terror of that horrible clamor in the forest. It had brought them closer together. Even if nothing practical had come out of it, though the suggestions had been—nearly all of them—robbed of virtue by the lack of tools, the conversation had heartened them to endeavors, roused their various ambitions, started the chain of ancient memories revolving the cogs of progress.

The association of ideas was milling in his own mind, tales read in his youth of the pioneers—a curious jumble—deadfalls—jerked beef and venison—the old *boucan* meat of the pirates of the Spanish Main. That last leaped on to the adventures of Bartholomew Portuguese escaping from the Spaniards, their Indian slaves and their bloodhounds.

Bartholomew had found a piece of timber beside a river, and the buccaneer, who could not swim, esteemed it a gift from the gods, for the timber had nails in it from which he contrived edged tools, whetting them on stones, and so felled trees and made him a raft on which he crossed the turbulent Cuban river and defied the alligators.

They must have been spikes rather than nails, Brett fancied. Spikes of hand-wrought iron. There were nails in the fragment of boat which he had not forgotten to bring from the beach, the nails Walker wanted to make hooks out of. An ingenious man might use them for all sorts of useful purposes—as awls—to use in making sandals. Brett felt his imagination stirring. They were an average crowd of men such as you might find on a city street. No mechanics among them, none cunning in woodcraft, a Canadian *voyageur* would laugh at them for lost children.

But, in their brains was packed all sorts of information, filed away subconsciously, a great deal of it, read or listened to without thought of special reference or need—yet there—records that could be got at, he believed, by the right sort of correlation.

The moon had dropped behind the cone that now loomed dark and mysterious. The wind had entirely died. There was a distinct drop in the temperature. Brett felt that dawn was close at hand though the stars were still effulgent, golden. Already he sensed subtle instinct quickening. Civilization's shell was peeling. He was becoming more natural, a comforting conviction was mounting within him that he could overcome all obstacles.

Malone was making them laugh.

"What would I know about the woods?" he asked. "Sure I'm a water rat. I was a wharf rat to begin with, back in New York, and I've lived my life in ships. Working like a dog in the furnace room an' gittin' me a thirst I c'ud niver git rid of when ashore. Me an' The Slovak, we're two of a kind, we are. Picnics, is ut, an' clambakes you're talkin of? Free lunch was more in our line 'till they amended 'em out of the Constitushion.

"Faith, if I had materials, I c'ud show you how to make a brand of hooch that 'ud send your troubles flyin' but I niver saw a bird's nest in my life, let alone robbed one. I'm with O'Neill, I'm a free Irishman an' the sooner I'm shook of this blasted island—if it is an island—the better it suits me. How about it, Wolf, what do you know about fishin' and huntin'? Spake up an' spill your wisdom."

Wolf turned his eyes toward Malone for a moment and they caught the fire again, glowing like those of the brutes that had glided through the brush. Then he resumed his position, staring into the night, listening, hugging his knees. There was something curiously alien about him that communicated itself to all of them.

"He was always a queer one," said Malone, discussing him as if he was absent, or a lay figure. Somehow this mode of speech seemed appropriate. "He'd not talk to a soul for a week at a stretch," went on Malone. "MacLeod, the second engineer, said he was a warlock—an' the oilers swore he brought on the storm. Somethin' missin'." He tapped his forehead significantly. Wallaby Brown threw more wood on the fire.

"Getting chilly," he said. And shivered. In the east the sky was lightening to gray. A dim glow showed behind it like the fire showing through the ash of a reviving ember. Rapidly it strengthened, turned to crimson, then to orange. All about them objects took on shape and color. In the woods a bird called to the dawn.

"You, oh you!"

CHAPTER V.
BIRD ISLAND.

THEY WERE a jaded lot in the sunshine, their flesh blistered and swollen with mosquito bites, treading on tender soles, what clothes they had in sorry condition, hair disheveled and beards sprouting. Walker voiced it.

"A 'appy band of 'oboes, we look," he said. "W'ot price a cup of corfee? At Lockhart's, in London, before the war, you could get a mug of cocoa, three thick slices of bread and butter—door-steps, they used to call 'em—for thrippence. A kipper or 'addie from thrippence up, 'cordin' to size. Then there was 'Arris'—Sausage an' Mashed, Thrippence. Veal and 'am pies fourpence. Extra large pork pies sixpence. Down Shaftesbury Havenue, the fried-fish shops. A 'unk of 'ake or flounder for tuppence. A chunk of thick peas-pudden for a penny, cup of corfee a penny, baked pertater a penny.

"W'ot'll you 'ave, gents? We've got hoysters fresh, boiled or broiled, hoysters fried and hoysters on the 'arf shell. Pick 'em off the ruddy trees like cherries. Sea fruit! Oo's coming with me to gather breakfast?"

Somebody threw a chunk of wood at him, which he dodged. Malone made a rush for him, joined by Tully, Bowman and Wallaby Brown. Walker skipped out of reach, his shoes taking him blithely where they could only hobble. The skylarking action broke up the general lethargy, abolished any atmosphere of self pity. Brown picked up short sticks and hurled them with wonderful accuracy at the steward until the latter hid back of a big rock and cried for truce.

Brett wondered whether Walker had not created the diversion purposely. That was one of the chief aims of a ship's steward, to cheer up the crestfallen, divert their attention from their own troubles. And Walker had been a good steward.

The professor was smiling at the chase though the smile had little gaiety or spontaneity and he made no attempt at movement, however slight. Brett walked over to him, regarding him anxiously.

"I want you to play fire-tender, professor," he said. "We'll get up some wood for you. Just stick around camp and take it easy. You'll have two assistants so all you have to do is to boss the job. We'll scare up some eggs and fish and we'll have some real food by nightfall. I don't believe there's any danger from wild animals by daylight. We'll hunt up some sort of a cave-dwelling before dark and establish ourselves."

Professor Harland nodded.

"That will be fine," he said huskily.

"How are you feeling?"

"Quite fit. Don't bother about me, Brett. I'm a little stiff, that's all. Egad"—he chuckled—"I rather wish Brown had hit Walker, not too hard, with one of those sticks he threw. We are creatures of habit and I must confess that my morning cup of coffee was a thing I had come to look forward to as a necessity." Brett nodded.

"And I would give all the oysters in the world right now, with the pearls that might be inside of them, for one sack of Durham and a pack of papers. But we must eat and oysters are the most available. Perhaps we'll have an omelet for supper. Roasted eggs, anyway. One thing I am quite sure of, that we are going to be able to make ourselves fairly comfortable with our united capacities and energies."

"Under your leadership—"

A call came from Walker, who had been exploring along the bank of the stream. He beckoned and stooped over something he was examining closely.

"Tracks!" he exclaimed as they hurried up. "Where they crossed the stream last night. Whoppers. Look at 'em." The impressions consisted of five pad-prints apiece, clustering to form a sort of rosette. Each pad was nearly as large as a dollar. Walker tucked in the first and second joints of his fingers and applied his hand, palm down. It barely covered a track. They were plain in the sand, emphasized by the shadows; and the sight of them brought back the pandemonium of the middle night, something of the prickling, chilling sensation of dread. They stood gazing in silence. Here was a menace that must be mastered.

Brett's thought went farther. Beyond the mastery lay reward. The threat of a capricious, rainy climate was steadily haunting him. Beasts boasting tracks like these, however formidable, once conquered, would furnish hides and furs, leather for multitudinous purposes, robes for clothing. It meant footgear, the bones could be made up into fishhooks, into knives. Once established in some secure dwelling, with the food problem solved, or partly solved, they must bend their energies to the destruction of these brutes, if not their entire extermination, which might not be wise, the intimidation of any remainder. The lines flashed up:

> *I am monarch of all I survey,*
> *I am lord of the fowl and the brute.*

That was what must be accomplished. Nature was provident enough; but she demanded tests for the survival of the fittest. Unconsciously Brett's lean jaw stuck out with the muscles bunching about it, his eyes narrowed and lines furrowed above them. Walker looked up at him approvingly. The ex-soldier knew men when he saw them; he recognized in Brett the executive who could rise to the occasion, however unequipped.

"Looks like it might be a lion," said Tully in a low voice. Brett was inclined to agree with him though he realized his utter ignorance of trail—spoor, as the big-beast hunters called it.

"Looks more like a dog to me," said O'Neill.

"Some dorg! I never saw a dorg big as those looked last night.

W'otever they are I'm going to keep my eyes peeled and stay in the open," said Walker.

"They made their kill last night, whatever they were," said Brett. He was trying to gauge the noise they had made. Lions roared and coughed, he had read. Some dogs bayed; some howled. The sounds might have fitted hound or lion, to his thinking. The gliding forms had been vague but he was fairly certain he had seen no manes. Cougars did not have ruffs.

He realized with a precise certainty that he must abandon his old-time habits of speculation. He was no longer living life at second-hand. What was needed from now on was quick decision—action—the throwing off of everything superfluous to the immediate issue.

"They'll likely lie up by day," he added. "The tide should be running out and the oysters exposed. Let's fill up on oysters and get a start for the island before the ebb turns. If we can judge the flow we'll have the flood to help us coming back. Malone, will you stay here with the professor and Wolf? The rest of us will get the shells. Walker, you might range a bit. There may be berries, or some sort of edible fruit. I don't believe there's much danger—and you've got shoes."

"Don't you worry about me."

They shoved off their catamaran with a sort of platform at one end made of broken boughs, slightly interlaced, thickly strewn with ferns to lay the shells upon. Malone started the ember fire beneath the cooking stone. Wolf stood looking on at the preparations without sign of interest. Brett did not speak to him. He figured that rest might reassert his balance. Meantime Malone could handle him better than anyone else.

"Isn't there something I can do?" asked Professor Harland.

Brett nodded. He looked for and found the fragment of boat planking. "These nails are our treasury, Mr. Harland," he said. "We could get them easily by burning the wood but that might destroy the temper. It is fairly soft lumber. You might try to get the nails loose. There are seven of them. The wood will splinter, I think, if you hammered it with this chunk of flint. Don't get too strenuous. There's plenty of time."

He felt it imperative to find tasks for the professor to prevent the scholar from feeling himself too impotent. He judged him by himself. If Harland became imbued with the idea that he was done up he might let down too far for recovery. He did not imagine he would do much with the nails, but there was no doubt that the professor brightened as he took the bit of plank.

Whatever their latitude might be, there was no doubt as to the strength of the sunlight. The rays began once more to inflame their blistering flesh. The boat trip had somewhat weathered them, but the one day on the beach had for the first time caused them actually to suffer. Wrists and foreheads and necks were in worst shape though lips were cracked and noses red and swollen. The flesh was tender, spongy. Brett remembered Crusoe's umbrella. Better parasols, he fancied, could be made from leaves on some sort of a light frame.

One of the first things they must contrive was some substitute for string to bind such things together. For the present they made chaplets of ferns, plaiting them roughly and setting the crude contrivance on their heads, letting the fronds trail down. For the exposed limbs there seemed no remedy. Sooner or later the skin would harden, he supposed.

The tales of travel he had edited, the yarns of castaways, usually avoided such painful details, the minor irritants of adventure. He grinned to himself, poling along, astride one of the logs, thinking of his ability to write a realistic story—with what—on what—for whom to read? It was a far, far cry from their ocean wilderness to the land of printing presses and newsstands.

It took longer than they expected to gather a sufficient supply of oysters. The ebb was not sufficiently advanced and they had to wait. Poling back against the stream was difficult work this morning. Brett was so stiff in every aching joint he wondered they did not creak to his movements.

They returned to find Walker triumphant. He had discovered a thicket of luscious berries, larger than blackberries, full of flavor and sweet. He had contrived a crude basket from fern fronds, lining it with large leaves and had brought back a plentiful supply. Wolf sat stolidly by the side of the stream, Malone beside him. The professor had pounded and splintered the boat fragment successfully to release the nails. Walker had a bit of the wood in his hand with a nail in it forming an acute angle. The steward showed it to Brett as they shared the berries, while the oysters were roasting.

"I can smooth down the wood a bit with some of that rock down by the stream," he said. "Reg'lar pummy-stone it is. It'll make the shank of a hook and the nail'll do the trick. I can rub the point sharp though we'll 'ave to forget a barb. There's fish in that stream—big 'uns in the pool—rising—see that one."

A big fish had risen to some insect and, for a second, exposed part of a silvery body. "Carnt fly-fish for that beggar. But I can get 'im bottom fishing. A pole, this 'ook, a bit of dry wood for float, hoyster bait—or mebbe I can find wigglers under the flat stones—and part of Mr. O'Neill's pajammer cord for line and we're set. Bet I catch one before you go. If I do you better let me put in the day fishing. You'll find those birds' eggs tasting like train-oil. Ought to be eels in the tidewater and I can get them without any 'ook at all."

"Spear them, you mean?" Walker was showing up well, Brett thought.

"Spear nothink! Where 'ud I get a spear? See that tossel at the end of O'Neill's cord—two of 'em. Two more on Wallaby's. Untwist 'em and they're floss silk. Dig up some worms, tie 'em on the tossel in a big bunch, tie on your line, weight it. The eels'll go for 'em and their teeth'll stick in the floss. If you know 'ow, you can snake 'em out before they let go. Trouble'll be to handle 'em, 'thout a basket to put 'em in. Bet I'll have a mess of 'em for supper. You 'and me over your pajammer cord, O'Neill."

"Sure," said O'Neill sarcastically, "if you'll trade me a couple of safety pins for it."

"I'll divvy with you," put in Wallaby. "Mine's thick enough for two." Brett thought of his money belt. It had three buckles on it. It was useless for its original purpose and it could be ripped up into strips, part of it making a belt for O'Neill, the rest of it put to many uses. If they only had a knife. A flake flint substitute would be a poor one, taking time, probably long practice to perfect.

He took off his belt and the money from its pockets. The others looked at it with some slight interest. Wolf alone regarded it greedily.

"Not much use here," said Brett with a laugh. "But we ought to be able to do things with the belt. You take it to hold up your lowers, O'Neill. I'll stow this cash away somewhere. The gold is metal. It may come in handy if we are able to melt it down. You've got pockets in your trousers, Professor, I wish you'd take care of this for me."

He made up the currency into a slim roll. Wolf's covetous eyes never left it. Professor Harland opened the roll, counted it.

"Eleven hundred dollars," he announced.

"Correct," said Brett. "Purchasing power nil. Here's two hundred in gold, a little more valuable. Represents my capital, all of which I would gladly swap at this minute for a good knife and a sack of tobacco."

"I'd give twice that, if I had it," said Malone, "for a slab of chewin' and ha'f a pint of whisky. 'Speshully the whisky. I sure need a drink worse than I ever did in my life—with less chance of gettin' it."

"Oysters are ready," Brett announced. "Pick 'em as they open. Here's your belt, O'Neill. We may need some of it back after a while."

The professor ate several oysters thoughtfully. "Not a bad breakfast," he said finally. "I have been wondering what crude races do for string and rope. There is some long-stemmed grass over there that seems fairly strong. Perhaps it could be plaited."

"They make sennit," announced Walker. "Three-ply braided up from palm fiber or from stringy bark stuff. Sailors make it from grass and straw for hats. Natives use the three-ply plait to make up bigger ropes. I ain't seen any palm trees so far and I don't know what kind of bark they use. But they 'ad to find it out and we ought to be able to."

"We've got a lot to find out," said Tully. "Our brains ought to be as good as a savage's. There are sinews and guts we could use. And there's the *tapa* cloth they wear. Isn't that material made from the inside bark of a tree?"

"Paper mulberry," answered Brett. Odds and ends of what he had read were forming in line now. "They soak it and pound it with clubs. I wouldn't know a paper mulberry if they grew here but there may be other trees with the same sort of inner bark. Like birch. It's a matter of experiment. We'd better be starting after the eggs before the ebb gives out. Walker, you're going to fish. Professor, you'll stay in camp and watch the fire. Wolf, will you come for eggs with us?"

It was the first time he had spoken directly to Wolf since he had noticed the change in him. The oiler did not show any signs that he had heard. Malone slapped him on the shoulder and repeated the question. Wolf suddenly bounded to his feet, a rock in one hand and stood snarling, his eyes blood-shot.

"Better lave him alone a bit," said Malone. "He'll sleep it off. Maybe I'd better stick around and keep an eye on him."

"All right. Five of us are enough to handle the raft. Some day we'll manage a canoe and paddles."

"Some day? You talk as if we were here for the rest of our lives. How long do you suppose we'll have to stay here before we are taken off?"

O'Neill spoke petulantly. It was the first time the thought that had been in all their minds was openly broached. They looked at each other.

"You know as much about it as I do, O'Neill," Brett answered. "I don't know where we are. We may even be on the mainland, though I doubt it. We may be somewhere near the regular route of ships. If we are not taken off in that way we shall have to stay here until we can manufacture tools, first of all, and then build a seaworthy craft."

"A fat chance we'd have of making land," said Bowman. "We don't know which way to go to hit the nearest land. It may be thousands of miles away. We haven't any compass, we can't navigate. A fat chance! To make a start from nowhere to some place unknown!"

"Just as fat a chance of building a boat without nails or an ax or even a knife. What'll we do for sails—row the thousands of miles? We've got as much chance of getting off this place as they have of serving ice-cream in — !" Bowman's voice was bitter. He slumped dejectedly on a log. "Look at us," he went on. "A fine bunch we are, a helpless, hopeless lot of cast-aways without clothes or weapons, trapped here, cut off from life—from everything—like—like—!"

"A group of fleas afloat on a shingle!" Wallaby Brown laughed at his own metaphor. It was a hearty laugh, good to hear, somehow warming. "I don't look at it that way," he went on. "Men 'ave been shipwrecked before and come out all right. We're a blamed sight better off than we were last night. We've got fire and grub, we ain't going to starve. You said something about our brains being better than a cannibal's just now, Tully. I don't bank much on mine but I do on Mr. Brett's there.

"We've got along so far and we'll get along all right for grub and clothes and we'll build a boat if we have to. One thing's sure, it's no use bellyaching about it. Quitting in the first round before you get warmed up. There's the professor. Old enough to be the daddy of any of us, to be your granddaddy, Bowman—without offense to you, professor. He's forgot more'n you've learned. Lived in a city all his life, likely. Ain't used to roughing it. Misses his cup of coffee and his pipe and morning paper and all the rest of the things a blamed sight more'n you do. 'Aven't heard a whimper out of *him*. Game, 'e is. Lord, you've got all your limbs and your eyesight, ain't you? You can see and smell and hear and walk and you're full of breakfast. What more do you want?"

Walker put down the tackle he had been fussing over.

"That's the way to talk," he cried. "I don't know if you boys went overseas or not. I did. I've lived knee-deep in mud and blood, I 'ave, slept in a funk-hole and seen the gas comin' down the wind after we'd been sprayed with shells for 'arf the day. I've lived on emergency rations with the fear of Gawd in my empty belly, prayin' I'd be wounded and git a chance at Blighty. I've gone over the top with the machine guns bowlin' us over like ninepins. I 'ad three years of that, off and on, and this plyce is a ruddy bit of Paradise beside that, sonny. You don't know when you're well orf. Are we down 'earted? *No!* Now I'm going fishing. This, w'y this is a bloomin' picnic!"

"You're right, Walker," said Tully, his face reddening for all the sunburn. "I had no call to grouch. I saw a bit of the other side. So did Bowman. I reckon we'll make out somehow."

Walker turned and grinned on his way to the pool. "Now you're talking. Cheerio!"

"It isn't the luxuries," said O'Neill. "Or the—danger. I mean from those brutes we heard last night. It's having a slice cut out of your life. After a man has worked up to where he begins to taste success—"

Malone interrupted him. There was friction between the oiler and the film star that Brett fancied was deeper rooted than any cause growing from Malone's resentment of the actor's occasional flashes of implied superiority.

"Missin' the sweeties an' the mashnotes, O'Neill—if that's your name? Missin' drivin' up in the swell car an' dollin' up in the fine clothes to peacock in front of a camery? Thinkin' you'll not be pullin' down the big salary by the time you get back? Fearin' the girlies will forget how handsome an' brave ye are? There's no stars an' no supers here, my bucko. We'll all be eatin' equal an' workin' equal, I'm thinkin'."

O'Neill stood with clenched fists, dramatically posed, his eyes flashing with rage. He turned on his heel as Malone snickered and strode off among the ferns.

"There's small sense in stirring up trouble, Malone," said Brett. "We've got enough on our hands as it is. We've got to all pull together."

He spoke sharply. The authority in his voice surprised himself somewhat. Malone whirled, his face ugly with temper. Wallaby Brown came closer to Brett. Tully and Bowman ranged themselves with him.

"Figgerin' to boss the crowd?" asked Malone. "Got a majority all ready? Listen, you may have been travelin' first-class aboard the steamer but this is another sort of boat we're in. Why, for two cents I'd—"

Brett went hot with sudden rage as if his blood had suddenly risen to boiling point. His fists balled. Reason he set aside and knew only an overpowering emotion to slug it out with Malone, regardless of the fact of physical discrepancy. He would be no match for Malone, rough and tumble fighter of groggery and fire-room. He shook off Brown's clasp on his arm. The sneer on Malone's face maddened him. He had never been in a fight since he was a boy. But he seemed to have suffered a sea-change, to have stepped entirely into the primitive.

A whoop from Walker saved the situation. A whoop followed by a mighty splash and a gurgling cry for help. They saw the steward up to his neck in water, one arm holding a limber pole that he had torn from a sapling. The impromptu rod was bent double, the line was taut. Circles distinct from those of Walker's making showed where a fish was on.

Then the fisherman's foot slipped and he disappeared. The pole was jerked from his hand and went sliding off, dragged now and then beneath the surface. Brett made a running dive and, as his head broke water, he saw Walker once more on his feet, sputtering, gesticulating.

"Get 'im, guv'nor! Get 'im! 'E's still on. Swim after it. A whacker, 'e was. There's no barb on that hook. Don't lose 'im!"

Brett struck out after the pole, grasped it and swam on to the far side of the pool where he got foothold on some shelving rocks. Walker was jumping up and down in his excitement, shouting directions. Everyone but O'Neill was on the bank watching, enthusiastic, everything forgotten in their sporting instinct.

"Don't play 'im, guv'nor. Don't give 'im any slack. 'Old 'im! 'Old 'im tight! It's fair in 'is ruddy jaw. I'm coming over."

Walker ran for the rocks forming the lower end of the pool, leaping along them, making a jump across the channel, landing safely, arriving breathless beside Brett. The fish was swimming strongly at the end of the makeshift tackle, showing a broad side of silver occasionally. Brett stood braced with the butt of the pole in both hands. It bent ominously, it cracked, it sagged.

The gallery broke out into volleys of advice. O'Neill had come out of the ferns and stood with the rest, intent on the battle. It was not a question of the food supply but purely sporting instinct that had brought even Wolf back to normal for the moment. Walker was in the water, stooping, arms extended.

"Git 'im in, guv'nor, haul 'im in and I'll stick my fingers in 'is gills! The rod's going, grab the line!"

Brett reached for the line, reached it, hauled. The big fish came slowly, fighting back, inch by inch to where Walker stood on a rocky shelf on the verge of deep water with fingers hooked waiting to grasp it by the gills. Then came a churning flurry, a furious fighting of broad pectoral fins. The softer cartilage of the fish's cheek gave way, showing a ragged hole. With a groan from Walker, echoed by Brett, they saw the wooden shank of the hook slide down this gap to the jawbone and then come clear while the fish went plunging away and suddenly dived to the cool depths from which it had been lured.

The hook came in, the nail still in the wood but no longer at an angle. The weight of the fish and its struggles had straightened it. Walker cursed softly.

"It wasn't your fault, guv'nor," he said. "Might have landed a smaller one. C'ud 'ave got this one if I'd 'ad a landing net. That's just what I'm going to make me before sundown."

"You're going to hunt a cave for us as well as fish, Walker," reminded Brett. "You've got the only shoes. I'm going to try and make some sandals from bark but they won't last long. We may need them on the rocks."

"I'll hunt your cave and make that net too, don't you worry."

Brett felt certain that the net would be made. And that many other things they needed would be made in the same way. Walker's sporting blood was up, his interest aroused and his ingenuity would devise the tools he needed.

Brett walked over to the dike of obsidian that he had followed down through the woods to the stream. It was nearly black in color and of brilliant luster, resembling bottle-glass. His firestone he had pounded off but it did not provide what he was looking for, sharp edges that might be used for knives, that could slice through bark.

This rock was the stuff from which Indians made arrowheads and spearheads. He had seen such in museums, chipped so carefully that they were almost smooth, with barbs or with serrated edges. He had picked up cruder specimens on Mount St. Helena in Sonoma County, California. They had never struck him particularly as exhibits of skilled artificers but now he wondered how they had chipped the flint and remembered vaguely a statement issued by a Washington Bureau that the Indians had forgotten the art of making arrowheads.

There were fissures in the dike and in some places it overhung the main flow along the edges where it had cooled more rapidly. It struck him that he might affect cleavage of the mass if the stuff was heated and then had cold water poured on it, breaking it up into the splintery fractures characteristic of obsidian. If they were lucky they might find many frag-ments that could be used without shaping for various purposes. It was worth trying—later; they must not lose the ebb.

He called over Malone and suggested that he try the experiment. The sandals would have to go for the island trip. In time he supposed their feet would callous and harden like the feet of natives but the long soaking in the boat trip had made them more tender than usual. Still, the bulk of the trip to the islet would be by water and he imagined they could stand the inconvenience amid the excitement of getting eggs. He called the quartet up to get aboard the catamaran. Wallaby, Bowman and Tully came up with poles, launching the raft and wading out with it to the current.

"I'm not going," announced O'Neill.

"Why not?" Brett asked him. The film star shrugged his shoulders.

"I don't feel like it. I'm all fagged out."

"So are the rest of us." Brett's voice was crisp with the contempt he felt. He had no authority over O'Neill, for his implied leadership had not been definitely made. He had no right to command any of them.

"I don't see any sense in going after a lot of rancid eggs. Walker is going to get fish."

"He's going to do the catching and you the eating? Well, you've got a sweet nerve." O'Neill winced at Tully's caustic remark.

"Oh, I'll go," he said, wading out to the logs and taking a seat astride.

"It isn't only eggs I'm after," Brett explained as they swung downstream. "I saw a seal yesterday. Scared the daylight out of me at first. I made sure it was a cannibal. Seals may haul out, or whatever it is they call it, on that island. We may be lucky enough to club one—or more. The meat may be good chow and anyway the hide will give us leather."

They made the lagoon, paddling with their hands, timing their strokes, making fair progress. Presently the current Brett had noticed the day before gripped them and bore them toward the reef.

"How about sharks—outside?" asked Bowman.

"They say if you strike the surface the concussion will scare them away," said Brett. "So I've read."

"Looks as if we were going to prove up a good many story-book statements before we live here very long. All the same, I don't feel easy below the knees," said Bowman. Brett shared his sensation. They struck the water as they paddled with plenty of splash but the suggestion of insidious sharks gliding up and shearing off a leg was persistent and unpleasant. There were no triangular fins in sight. There were always fins showing above the surface before attack in all the stories Brett had edited or read.

Now he wondered whether sharks always swam that way before they bit a man. It did not seem reasonable that they would but rather that they would come sweeping up from below, silent and shadowy, planing on their powerful fins. Then they would roll over, their maws opening like crescents, armed with fixed, serrated teeth. *Scrunch!*

Imagination was hard at work with all of them and silence prevailed as, outside the reef at last, they paddled hard toward the islet. Myriads of birds were on it, undoubtedly watching them, unable to decide whether danger was connected with the object that moved closer to them with rhythmical movements.

Suddenly, with a roar of wings, a multitude of birds soared upward, wheeled in flocks, seaward, landward, flying in great circles that dipped so low and close they could see the open beaks, the beady eyes of the alarmed islanders while their cries were deafening, some querulous, some threatening and indignant.

There were gulls, slate and white, their tails rigid as the rudders of an aeroplane, tilting to guide the flight. There were birds with the beaks of eagles, brown of feather, with forked tails that closed and opened like scissors as they flew with enormous spread of wing.

There was one big cloud of shrieking protestants, white below and dark above with white collars, that were particularly vehement in their denunciation of the intruders. They had parrot-like beaks of great size, horny and corrugated, vividly colored in red and blue and yellow and there were scarlet horny projections above their eyes. These, passing so close to the raft that their flying shadow darkened it and the wind of their going was plainly felt, ranked up against the wind and then dived, to come up in a fussy fleet fifty yards away.

"Puffins," declared Tully. "I've seen them on Muskeget Islands off Nantucket. They nest in holes in the rocks and—glory, but they can bite with those beaks! Eggs taste like they'd been soaked in gasoline."

The islet was of porous rock that resembled pumice. Much of it was covered with bird droppings. It did not rasp their soles especially, for the waves and flying spray had smoothed the general surface that was pitted with holes just about big enough to admit hand and arm. The top was fairly level.

Here they found more birds, squatting and regarding the invaders uneasily but holding their ground though they scuttled off on close approach, revealing eggs on which they had been sitting. Some flew, more remained, crowding close to Brett and the others, even scuffing against their legs.

"First time they've seen humans," suggested Bowman.

"It can be the larst, far as I'm concerned," said Wallaby Brown. "I've smelled a few rotten things in my life, glue factories and slaughter-'ouses, but this 'as got them all backed up." The stench, under the hot sun, was nauseating. With it mingled the strong fumes of ammonia. The guano on which they trod was slimy, fetid stuff.

A bird, gathering courage, perhaps from desperation, pecked viciously at Tully's ankle as he stooped for eggs. The multitudes that had flown off at their landing were now hovering over the island. It looked as if they had taken counsel and resolved to protect their hatching grounds and drive off the wingless, giant bipeds. The clamor of their raucous cries was distinctly menacing.

"I don't believe I want any eggs," muttered Bowman. "I vote we get out of this. We're trespassers."

"I said there was no sense in the trip," said O'Neill. "Good Lord, here they come!"

The birds with the scissors'-like tails and the eagle beaks had marshaled forces into an angry company that came swooping back to their nesting grounds in desperate resolve to do battle with the invaders. They were frigate birds, fearless, and, their parental instinct aroused, aggressive and in deadly earnest. The rest of the winged army had assembled into squadrons, wheeling into formation with a precision that suggested council-of-war, premeditated fight under the direction of leaders skilled in warfare.

Like with like, the parrot-beaked puffins in one company, bosun's birds, terns and gulls and kittiwakes in others, screaming their war-cries, they made for the offenders, blinding them, smothering them, striking with keen beaks and rigid talons, registering sharp hits with their pinions, brushing softer plumage against the heads and hands of the shrinking men who buffeted vainly at this feathered multitude with little more effect than if the flying legions had been unsubstantial as a cloud, though armed with weapons that gouged and slashed and brought the blood. The humans, handicapped by the buffets of the swirling assailants, supremely at home in their airy element, stumbled over the guano-covered rocks, smashing scores of unprotected eggs, striving to protect their eyes rather than to take a negligible offensive against the intangible foe.

The puffins came into the fight on the flank—as it were. They alighted and waddled in interminable ranks to attack the feet and ankles of the would-be ravishers, each striving, scrambling to lunge with its great horned bill, staining its fantastic grooves a brighter scarlet than Nature had given it. The bites were dangerous, likely to be deadly. Blood spurted from broken flesh and severed veins, the gray-white guano was smeared with crimson in the over-trampled tracks. About the heads of the men was the constant buffet of wings, the whirr of fanning plumage, the hoarse cries of the birds. Every second a peck got home, a vicious stab or a scoring slash from armored claws.

Their wrists and hands were raw, their cheeks and brows laid open, the fern-frond makeshift hats torn away. Every attempt at open sight was an invitation to blindness. Ignorant of any danger, they had left their poles with the raft. Bowman slipped, staggered and went down, clutching at Tully, lugging him to the ground. Brett, peering from beneath crossed arms, saw a great group of the birds swoop down on the pair and cover them in a struggling mass, whose harsh screams sounded with a new note of triumph.

He caught sight of O'Neill, floundering close to a cliff-edge, bent almost double, his upper body almost concealed by the fluttering, raging birds. They were all near to a fall as they had retreated from the aerial attack without sense or thought of direction. Wallaby Brown was beside Brett and he flailed desperately with his arms beating off the soft, persistent bodies that were yet so rigidly boned of wing, so vindictively effective with their natural armament.

For a moment he was free and he plunged through the reassembling group, treading on the puffins regardless of their savage jabs, catching the prizefighter by the arm. Brown wheeled impatiently. Brett had a glimpse of his face, set in fighting mask but a mask that was bloody and freshly scarred. A bird dashed at its exposure and Brown clutched at it, caught it by the neck, swung it about until it was throttled with a defiant squawk and wings that slowly ceased to beat. Using the dead thing as a club, Brown swung it round in a circle, glaring again at Brett.

"W'ot in blazes," he demanded.

"Bowman's down—with Tully," panted Brett. "You're right at the edge, Brown. Look out! We've got to get them down to the raft."

His hope was the poles. The water-birds would likely continue the fight until they were well clear of the island. The cliff back of Brown was an almost sheer drop. Brett had lost all idea of direction. He did not know where to find the raft. But Bowman and Tully must be rescued. He had forgotten O'Neill.

Brown, swinging his bird, gained temporary clearance, saw the prostrate bodies indicated by the shifting mass of birds, puffins on the flanks, stabbing at legs and feet. He let out a yell and dashed forward, Brett with him. It was like fighting hornets. For one bird struck down as they strove to dash the mass aside, ten others came swooping in. They fought through a sea of them, the plumage for froth and spray, the compact bodies for the weight of water. Bowman and Tully lay on their stomachs, arms clasped around their heads, bloody from a myriad pecks. They were limp as Brett and Brown tugged at them; their arms hung down like lengths of rope; there was no strength to their legs.

A hoarse, appealing cry, that broke through all the clamor of the infuriated birds, the clan call of human to human, made them turn to where O'Neill in a flurry of wings, of striking necks, of black, beady eyes, went backward over the cliff with upflung arms.

They broke through the flying batteries, half dragging the two younger men. They pressed on, one arm free to beat off the frenzied creatures, struggling through the uproar and confusion to where the plateau top of the island grooved, led downward. Brett fancied this was the way by which they had climbed but his thoughts were fogged in dizziness, he was bewildered by the constant storm of blows; deafened, blinded, stumbling through the crowding, belligerent puffins, taking toll of blood and flesh at every step, smashing eggs that were rotten or half-hatched and whose stinking, sulfurous fumes mingled chokingly with the ammoniac stench of the slimy guano.

If he was wrong, they were done up. It would be the end and he was glad to know the finish one way or another. They were in the primitive, attempting life to sustain their own, fought for the same reason. Man against brute, brute against the man. And only a few hours back he had vaingloriously quoted—

I am lord of the fowl and the brute.

Down the pitch, blood and sweat in their eyes, Bowman and Tully moving like damaged automata, brakes on progress. O'Neill gone, blow after blow, more blood, blood spurting from a vein in Brett's foot, weakness coming, strength and will leaking—leaking—strength running out like water through a sieve. Harsh rock, ridges—Brown stumbling—Brett himself down on one knee—agony to rise!

Brown, with a burst of strength, erect with Tully in his arms. Shingle, slippery shingle, the buffet of wings, the cruel impact of beaks, talons in his hair—water—salt, stinging water, blessed as protection to his feet.

Fooled the puffins after all—no, curse them, they were swimming in platoons—where was Brown? *Crash!*

Brett, with the half-conscious Bowman, had pitched down into the shallows.

A hand gripped his shoulder, powerful, vital, bringing back his own abilities. The shock of the water helped. Brett got to his feet and stood drenched beside Bowman, arms about each other. For the moment the birds had ceased to attack, were wheeling uncertainly above the driven off raiders. And there was the raft with Tully seated on a log, swiping at the few birds within reach, a pole in both the hands that could hardly muster strength to lift it.

Splashing through the water, they reached the catamaran, shoved it off, menacing their assailants with the poles. The birds seemed to appreciate that their enemies had become more dangerous, that, since they were leaving them in triumphant possession, it might be as well to call a halt. Bowman and Tully collapsed, lying full length along the logs, hands and legs trailing in the water. Brett maintained himself erect with an effort.

There was something that had to be done—something. What was it? He looked at Wallaby, bathing his face. Bloody water dripped through his fingers. The backs of his hands were sliced. He was spattered with blood, his hair matted with it. His clothes—such as they were—were ripped, covered with slime. So with all of them—a quartet of retreating scarecrows. Lords of creation? Brett laughed, half hysterically. Brown gazed at him, startled.

"Licked to a frazzle by a lot of birds—five husky men. Where's O'Neill? He fell off the cliff. We've got to go after him."

"Needn't worry about him. He's spotted us. Swimming like a ruddy seal." Brown spoke jerkily, slobberingly. His mouth had been slashed by a beak and the lower lip hung in irregular halves. Brett followed the direction of his pointing finger and saw O'Neill. He had swum around a point of rock and he was making swift, clean progress with an overarm stroke toward the raft. A dozen birds flew low above him, scolding but not molesting. In a few minutes he had reached an outrigger to which he clung for a moment, avoiding Brett's eyes. Then he clambered out on the log between Bowman and Tully.

"We was just going to look for you," said Wallaby Brown, his voice charged with heavy sarcasm. "Didn't know that you could swim, Mister O'Neill. Nothing like learning 'ow in a 'urry when you 'ave to."

"I was sick yesterday morning, from the shellfish," said O'Neill. Then he countered. "Fine job we did, egg hunting. Lucky we're alive. You didn't happen to catch a seal or two, Brett?"

"I fancy that island is trespass proof. We made a mistake tackling the job but we've all of us got a lot of lessons to learn, I imagine."

"We've got one peach of a job right in front of us, before we make land, if we don't 'urry," said Brown. "Look at the sky."

The blue had all gone out of it, swiftly it seemed, though they had been too occupied to notice the weather. Now it was gray and greasy, the sea of the same hue and quality, with a nasty cross-jobble in it that worked the logs up and down and chafed the liana fastenings dangerously. The crater had turned slate color, the green of the trees had turned to almost black and the cliffs looked like rough-cast steel. The surf on the barrier reef had changed its not uncheerful drumming to a roar and the entrance to the lagoon was hard to pick out.

If Brett had not planned to catch the tide going and returning they could not have made it. As it was, the first grip of the flood appeared to be slowly tugging them toward it. A wind blew from the land, irregular, damp, chilling, bearing an earthy smell. The curious thing was that the waves, mounting in pyramids that tumbled to pieces rather than dissolved, threw off splatters of foam against the wind. It was phenomenal, the assembling forces of nature gathering ominously. Exhausted as they were, depression invaded them. The air was stifling, it affected them with its heaviness as if they had been deep-sea divers.

The wind no longer blew from the land. It came from the sea, from behind, from all quarters, back from the land again. And with it, or born of it, came a perpetual moaning sound, inexpressibly mournful and foreboding.

The gray and greasy sky slowly darkened. The crater stood out sharply with a steady play of flickering lightning back of it. Gradually sky and sea changed to an awful green, the green of corruption that comes on moldering meat. The wind began to blow steadily and the jobbling seas heightened. The source of the storm seemed, to Brett's feverish imagination, vested in the crater, as if a malignant god of the winds was seated there in some cavernous split, blowing at them, keeping them off the land in devilish malice. Human conceit in the face of all elementary manifestation suggested that they were the victims upon whom all this increasing display of force and wrath was centered.

Despite the wind, the inflowing tide, obeying its law, unmindful of surface agitation, set them mercifully down toward the reef gate. The catamaran swung along the spouting barrier, lurching toward destruction with the sweep of the waves, thrust off desperately by their poles which they set against the submerged coral. The high-flung surf showered down on them like a Niagara. At the break they swirled in an eddy, grating, tilting, through to smooth water—comparatively—though even the lagoon was being whipped to choppiness.

The sky was green-black now, like the trees. The whole world, sky and sea and land, was either green-black or deep purple, the color of fresh-fractured slate. There was no effect of clouds but a feeling as if the half dome of the sky had been reduced to a quarter, diminishing the air supply, threatening to crush them. And the tortured air groaned and wailed in its compression.

Suddenly, without thunder, the crater leaped out, clear, living, every seam and rift of the mountain distinct under a lurid light that spread from back of it as swiftly, almost as dazzlingly, as if an inconceivable quantity of magnesium had been ignited. In the glare, spectral, showed for the first time speeding hosts of dark cloud about whose edges played a selvage of lavender lightning. They vanished with the boom of thunder. It crashed about them, shattering the universe. All things were blotted out.

It was near noon but they were in darkness as great as that of a total eclipse. Out of the sky, as if it had floored a lake, the bottom of which had collapsed, torrents of water came hissing, flooding down, the imminent clatter of it drowning out all other sounds, dominating the senses. The force of it literally beat them prostrate. Between lagoon and rain they were almost aswim, breathing water.

It was the current, taking them along as a carrier belt bears the factory product, that alone made it possible for them to fetch the mouth of the stream. The rain had lightened the intense blackness, diluted it to dark gray but they could see nothing beyond three feet, nothing beyond their logs but down-rushing, upspouting water.

It had rained hard when they were in the boat, but nothing like this. The streams of water, falling from unguessable height, hurt them as distinctly as the blows of a thick lash. Once Brett scooped up some water and tasted it, suspecting they were in the river. It was brackish and he knew. The catamaran bucked under them, threatening to come apart. At the bend where the stream came down from the canon there was always an eddy. Now it might be dangerous unless they could forestall the peril with their poles.

Whether their pupils became adjusted to the gloom or the latter was still diminishing as the cloud reservoirs slowly emptied, objects became remotely visible. Mangroves, the loom of the crater's lower slopes, rushes. They had come to the turn and the tide still had them. All about the hissing river, rain coming down in gray rods, mangroves showing vaguely—they looked in vain for the signs of camp. That the fire could have been maintained in such a deluge seemed inconceivable. Their progress could not be observed even though their comrades had not sought such shelter as they could find.

Tidal water reached as far as the waterfall. Into the basin at its foot they were barred entry by a low cascade pouring through a narrow pass. Reaching this they would know themselves at the end of the trip, but by no other means in that welter of water.

They arrived at the pool, sodden, exhausted. Bowman and Tully had revived only enough to sit bedraggled astride their logs. O'Neill was in better shape despite his fall. Wallaby Brown did most of the necessary poling though Brett stuck with it. But there was no cascade. The river had swollen. Through the pelter of the rain they heard the thunder of the augmented waterfall.

The brown water, stained by dirt in solution, was scummed with thick yellow froth, whipped by the downpour and the violence of its own impeded rush. Several times they had run on to submerged rocks that showed they were out of the main course as they had known it. Tide met torrent in a whirlpool where they were helpless as a beetle dropped from a bough into a river.

Brett shouted, then Brown, but the veil of rain muffled their efforts. The Professor, Wolf, Malone—whom Brett had designed more as bodyguard for the professor than warder of Wolf—before it was decided Walker should stay to fish and search for a cave—all were swallowed up, vanished. Somehow Brett pinned his faith on Walker, expected to see him, to hear him announce results. He was a resourceful chap, was the steward and ex-soldier. But the storm had come up with practically no warning.

They were horned on a dilemma, without food, fire or refuge. The rain was warm; so was the water, but it lowered their vitality, slowed the flow of blood, pinched and wrinkled the flesh and beat on their spirits with its inexorable force. It was getting dark again, there was no sign of a let-up, rather of an increase. The chance of light or sun before night fell was remote.

There came a halloo, faint but shrill, in answer to their strained shouts. It issued from the bank opposite to the camp. Swept in an eddy toward it they poled desperately and achieved a backwater, blundered into some half submerged bushes, grasped them, pulled themselves onward and became aware of Walker, in water up to his waist.

" ——'s nyme!" he cried, wading out to catch hold of an outrigger that parted under the strain just as they felt gravel underfoot and started toward him. "I thought you beggars were drowned or swept out to sea. I didn't know w'ot to do. Afraid I'd miss you. I've found a cave—a good one, though it's a bit of a scramble.

"We was moving in when the bottom fell out of the ruddy sky. Saved a bit of fire—the prof did that. Saw the sky darkening an' acted prudent. Malone an' that dumb Finn, or whatever he is, hauled up wood. None too much of it. You'll 'ave to foller me close. I think I can find the way. I've been roosting between two stones an' I've kept fairly dry. I ain't now. You didn't bring any eggs, I suppose?"

"No eggs," said Brett. "We're a henpecked crowd, Walker."

"Fair done in," added Brown. Walker whistled dolefully.

"We're going shy on grub if this rain keeps up long. Looks like a reg'lar forty-day-and-nighter, w'ot? I got a bunch of eels and five good-sized fish like the one we lost, on'y not so big. But we didn't 'ave time to grab any oysters an' we won't get any now. Not unless you dived for 'em.

"The water's risin' fast. Lucky my cave was high up, as it turned out."

He did all the talking during the stiff clamber over sliddery earth and rock, the ground dissolving under their feet in mud on the slopes and the rain shooting down, wrapping everything in obscurity. It had all the force of a high-pressure needle shower. If it had not been coming down in sheets but in fine lines of spray Brett fancied it might have drawn blood.

He believed it came close to bruising. It thoroughly cleansed their cuts and the clay with which their feet was plastered was comforting if not curative.

"'Ere we are," announced Walker when it seemed to all of them they would drop from fatigue. "Stairs to your right. No lift. I lugged over that dead tree an' propped it up. May 'ave to use it for firewood. But you ain't going to 'ave to worry about the lions."

The bark still clung scabbily to the slanting tree up which they clambered lamely to the gaping mouth of an opening in a cliff wall to the base of which they had climbed up a steep, unplanted pitch. Bowman went first, then Walker, boosting him. Tully followed with Brown assisting; Brett last.

Inside a fire shone ruddily in a glorious welcome. Red ashes shone under a little altar erection, on the top of which the professor was tending something that smelled royally. Malone helped them over the threshold. Wolf sat squatting back of the fire, arms wrapped round his knees, his face full, not lifting to greet them, his eyes shining in the glow.

"Some dugout? A little bit of all right, eh? And the fish done to a turn. I'm saving the eels. They'll keep 'emselves fresh. 'Ard to kill. We've got fern for beds an' it's dry in 'ere anyway. Don't smell like a scent-shop but that'll pass off. Bats—millions of 'em. Nearly knocked me over, them and their smell. Git close an' dry off. ——'s nyme, who's bin chewin' you?"

Walker kept up his cheery chatter while they stripped and stood about the life-giving fire. He hung their pitiful garments up on the driftwood that had been carried in, a pile that did not seem capable of lasting many hours. But they did not discount their blessings. They were dazed with weariness, with hunger. The fire showed rough projections of lava for walls and roof; it hinted at shelves, at inner hollows and chambers; it disclosed columnar stalactites reaching down; and it gleamed in the solid downpour of rain that curtained the entrance like a flawed mirror. The cavern was apparently a blowout of lava, rent by exploding gases. It was also a House of Refuge.

There were pits on the projecting lip of the threshold into which the rain sloshed and these were their drinking cups. The fish were charred in spots or else half raw, they were bonier than shad, muddy-flavored as carp and they were unscaled. But hunger was the sauce or, rather, exhaustion condoned the lack of it. They slumped at last into their beds of fern, naked, lying close as the dampness of the cave interior broke their sleep, digging into the mass of fronds as dogs would, stiff and sore but drugged with slumber.

Brett awakened once. Whether it was midnight or whether the hidden sun rode somewhere back of the rain-veil he could not tell, barely conjectured. The fire was low, a mass of glowing ashes. He started to summon his will to arise and replenish it when he saw a moving figure place a log on the embers, then another. The light showed the half sardonic grin that was Walker's habitual expression. Brett relaxed thankfully, falling asleep again to the persistent slosh of the rain, beating on their stone threshold, pouring down outside with a steady, settled rush.

There was no need of defenses against wild beasts. There were no hunting packs abroad. All living things sought their habitations save those belonging to the element that was, for the time, supreme.

CHAPTER VI.
WAYS AND MEANS.

THE NEXT DAY passed without hint of sun, with no view from the cave but the vertical warp of rainfall, none inside but the surfaces that caught the fire, niggardly fed with the rapidly vanishing fuel, and the deep shadows. Walker adventured into the torrent and came back with some indifferent clay which he used to envelop his eels before baking them in the ashes.

The dampness mocked the fire, the smell of bat-dung seemed accentuated by it. They crouched about the flame, turning themselves as if they had been roasts on automatic spits, miserable, sinking low in the scale of humanity, save for their qualities of thought. And thought was not pleasant.

Walker reported that the water had risen far up the slopes. Until it should subside they had no chance of getting oysters, no hope for fishing. All loose timber, much that was now being uprooted, would be carried down to the lagoon and out to sea to drift along in the coast current. Some they would eventually retrieve but it would be sodden, it would take hours even of that fierce sun to render any of it fit for firewood.

If—and this was the main fear that haunted Brett—if they had arrived at the commencement of a rainy season there was no telling how long this weather would last. They could not survive very many days of it. They could make two small meals of the eels or they could eke them out for four or five. By that time the fire would be gone. His imagination conjured up a pile of skeletons, of moldering bones, lying undiscovered until their chemical constituents resolved themselves into the floor dirt.

The professor would be the first to go but the rest would not long survive him. To adventure outside was madness, to stay was slow decay, unless the weather changed. It was no wonder that primitive men worshiped the sun. To feel its rays permeating the sodden flesh, to bask in it, absorbing vitality, would engender thankfulness as to a god. As to the Great Being or Power that had conceived the balanced machinery of the universe, such a credence seemed very far off.

Brett was not an agnostic but his belief in a personal god dwindled. They were atoms, composed of atoms, doomed to chemical reactions, unconsidered dust on the great machine that relentlessly whirled on its cosmic mission.

The better part of him, the stronger, fought against this depression. That way madness lay. So savages gave up resistance and died. The silence that had settled on them all must be broken up. Not by discussion of their conditions; the outlook was too dreary. He had one ray of hope in a dim remembrance that equatorial islands were subject to unsettled weather without any definite seasons of wetness and drought.

The Galapagos, for instance, he had read—or so he thought—were subject to rains and fogs, with vegetation that did not conform with the general idea of the tropics. But his brain seemed torpid, he could not evolve certainty of memory.

He found himself puzzling over the reason why they had seen no coco-palms. Such trees he had considered universal in these latitudes. There might still be some, but the weather precluded adventuring. They did not yet know whether they were on the mainland or not. How coconuts would solve their problem! Meat in the pulp, refreshing drink, fire from the husks—but they would have a tough job to husk them.

It was hard to pursue any line of thought; his wits were wool-gathering. But he evolved a theory that coco-palms grew only where the floating nuts could land upon fertile soil, that an island where the beaches were mere stripes of shingle at the foot of high cliffs offered no opportunity for growth even if the currents were so set as to bring the nuts. As for the trees that were there, birds might have transplanted the seeds in their droppings or they might be on the relic of a continent that, subsiding, had left remnants of forests.

It was all idle conjecture, useless as the treadmill of a squirrel in its cage. But he was unable to herd his thoughts, the gloom, the damp seemed possessing him, seeping through his flesh, laying siege to his soul. A look at the faintly seen faces of the others, brooding, with vacant eyes and sagged jaws, showed that they too were succumbing to despondency.

He got up, rearranged the logs to conserve the heat, spurred himself to an effort.

"There's no sense to our glooming in this fashion," he said; and the rest started at his voice. "We've got to make the best of it until it quits raining. We need some sort of amusement. I suppose Noah and his family told tales in the ark. Some of us have had experiences worth while relating. Walker, how about you? You were in the war. I wasn't. Physical handicaps, including age. How about it?"

The steward, sitting next to Brett, stirred himself.

"Nothing about the war I want to talk about," he said. "Give you the 'ump to 'ear it. Over there? Stink—mud—blood—death——!"

He hunched down again, staring into the fire with eyes that seemed to sight scenes that hardened his face to a grinning mask. So he must have looked, squatting in the trench, waiting the zero hour, thought Brett.

"Walker's right," said Wallaby Brown. "I did my bit. You don't want to think about it, much less talk about it. Leastwise, I don't, and I never found any mates of mine who were in the thick of it that did. I ain't supposed to be what you'd call sensitive—being a prizefighter—but I'm for forgetting the war and my end of it. Ruddy murder and sudden death!

"I spitted one Heinie—in the guts. Faugh! Shooting's a clean death. Though I don't suppose I 'urt 'im much. He looked surprised, the beggar. A man one minnit—the next a lump of meat on a prong. No grudge between us but it was 'im or me. I'm through with war."

"I didn't see any of that," said Tully. It had not been a good beginning, Brett thought, but at least they were talking. "I was gassed. The next war won't see bayonets or rifles, to my mind. It'll be a war of the chemists. They'd only begun on them when the armistice stopped things. They talk of disarmament and they think of battleships and great guns. Take them all away from Germany and leave her her dye works and she can start up again any time. The last stage in making black dye for stockings is picric acid for bombs and shells. The last stage of a lot of dyes is T. N. T.

"Aeroplanes by the thousand and gases that'll kill a man a mile off or acids that'll send him west if two drops spill on him. They won't even have to make a hit on a ship carrying supplies or troops. As for a city, they can sweep over it at two hundred miles an hour, a mile high, and annihilate it. After I got so I could breathe and see, I read up all I could about it. Lewisite chemists'll run the next rumpus. Air raids in the middle of the night with the city asleep, and never waking up, if the enemy breaks through the ring of defending dirigibles and air scouts."

"We'll be out of it," put in O'Neill.

"Were you ever in it? The last one, I mean," jeered Malone.

"No. I couldn't pass the examination. Were you?"

"I was, my bucko. I was passing coal on a transport while you were screen-struttin'." O'Neill glowered at Malone and the fireman grinned back at him. On the other side of Malone Wolf sat, as if he had been carved out of a log.

"They kept me marking time in camp," said Bowman. "I haven't had much experience of excitement until now, if you call this exciting. I wish I could tell a story but I was never any good at that sort of thing. How about you, Mr. Brett, you're an editor."

"I was, for my sins. I've read thousands of stories, a few good, many indifferent and most of them bad. And forgot all of them as promptly as possible to leave my mind free, save as I filed away the outlines of their plots to avoid buying repetition. Storytellers are born, not made, I imagine. The tribes set great store by their tale weavers. An inherited gift, I fancy. I haven't got it."

"Is it a story you're wanting? I've heard many and told not a few," said Malone. "Here's one that's true and it happened to a pal of mine and myself in Manila———"

He went on with his tale, unvarnished, crude and bestial, boasting of his prowess in drunkenness and lechery.

"They're all alike, the women," he said, "white, yeller, brown and black. The next day—" He looked round for appreciation, sensed the lack of it, and sneered. "Maybe it's too red-blooded for ye? But it's life I'm tellin' you. It's——"

"It's plain muck; that's what it is, Malone."

Malone snarled at Brown.

"You?" he emphasized. "I thought you had some guts." And Brett saw that Malone, out of some form of resentment, had told the smutty yarn deliberately in the hope it would offend, getting some malicious pleasure out of that desire. There were peculiar twists and kinks in the oiler's way of looking at life, born of long, arduous, sweating hours in a ship's bowels, muscles racked at high temperatures, followed by the inevitable reaction of debauch. He was the victim both of circumstance and consequence.

"I've got guts enough," answered Brown. "That talk of yours makes 'em crawl. I don't suppose you've met a decent woman since you were a kid, Malone. When you say they're all alike, all like the kind you're talking of, you're insulting the good ones, to my mind, insulting all our mothers, to begin with, your own included—and I expect she was good to you, Malone.

"I'm by way of being what they call in the States a roughneck, but I've got a wife and a couple of kids I'm hoping to get back to some day and, the way we're fixed just now, not knowing if we're going to come out of it or not, your line of stories is muck. Lots of dirt is clean but some is filth. Wolf may stand for it but the rest of this crowd won't."

" —— !" ejaculated Malone. "Too bad you didn't happen to bring a Bible and hymn book along; you could have held a Sunday School class. You ought to bin a preacher 'stead of a fighter. A fine bunch of softies."

"You wouldn't find me so soft if you ever tackled me, Malone. And I can fight a —— sight better than I talk." There was a gloss of good humor still covering Wallaby's words. Brett fancied he would fight that way, keeping his anger simmering, under control, as an asset, good-natured in defeat or victory. Nevertheless he suggested purpose and strength. If he did not directly challenge Malone he drew a line beyond which it was policy for the oiler to stay unless he wanted to come to grips. And this he was not ready for.

"Aw, go hire a hall," he retorted. "Who asked you to do the talking for the crowd? They got tongues of their own."

"Brown said just what the rest of us were thinking, Malone, unless I'm very much mistaken. Majority rules, you know," said Brett.

"The —— it does! Because there happens to be seven of you Sweet Williams against the Slovak an' me, that don't change my way of thinkin'; it don't force me to play baby."

Nobody answered him and he subsided, growling to himself.

"I know a story," said the professor, diffidently. "It was set down a long time ago, almost two thousand years ago, and told of the wanderings of a hero and his band of heroes long before Virgil recalled the ancient legend. It tells of love and war and adventure and it is, to me, the greatest story, besides the greatest epic poem, ever produced. If you would care to hear it, as I have translated it—?"

The assent was cordial. Malone gave a noncommittal grunt; Wolf nothing. So it started, the story of Aeneas, told in the dark cave by the sick fire. The professor rolled off his beloved hexameters with deep feeling, colored by his own enthusiasm, hour after hour until his voice grew husky, his memory clear in reproducing his labor of love:

> *War is my song, and the man, who first from the Ilian seashore,*
> *Banished by fate, into Italy came, and Lavinian harbors;*
> *Long was he driven o'er land and sea by the fury of Heaven,*
> *Through the vindictive wrath of implacable Juno; afflicted*
> *Cruelly also by war, or ever he founded a city,*
> *Bearing his gods into Latium, whence the proud race of the Latin,*
> *Sires of the Alban town, and the city of Rome in her glory.*

Hour after hour, forgetting for the time hunger and all their discomfort, the miserable and suffering castaways listened to the declamation of the gentle New England scholar, his soothing voice dramatic as he told of shipwreck, of imperial Sidonian Dido and her passion for the stranger warrior, of the fall of Troy, of sports, and feasting, of battle, of struggle that was taken up by the gods, of Charybdis and the Harpies, of Cyclops and Polyphemus, mortals and immortals, Dido on her pyre, sinking on the steel——

With the blood foaming out round the dagger.

So, while the rain poured down unceasingly, they descended with Aeneas and the Sibyl into the region of shades, crossed the Styx with Charon, of terrible filth——

Polling his bark himself, he handles the sails unassisted,
While in his dusky skiff he ferries the dead o'er the river.

They saw Cerberus——

. . . stretching his monstrous bulk in an opposite cavern,
Making the regions resound with the noise of his three-throated howling.

With the Sibyl they flung to the brute——

. . . a sop imbrued with honey and somnolent juices.

They passed the Plain of Lamentations, they reached the Elysian fields and saw Aeneas embrace the shade of his father Anchises. They listened to the prophecy of the glories of Rome. The professor's voice faltered to a hoarse whisper as he came at last to the end of the sixth book and they realized how much they had drawn upon his strength for their own entertainment and oblivion from their troubles——

Anchor from prow is dropped, and the sterns are at rest on the seashore.

"There are six more books," said Professor Harland. "I think them best, though they are not commonly studied. But I shall have to leave them for tomorrow—unless I have been boring you."

The hearty denial cheered him and he nodded at them.

"Lessons there, for us," he whispered huskily.

"I'll say so," said Walker. "Some scrappers, those chaps. But they had their boats and their armor. When they were shipwrecked they had their weapons. And the Dido dame served them up a banquet. We're worse off than a bunch of savages, we are."

"How do you make that out?" asked Bowman.

"Well, first place, a savage knows how to make the best of what things are 'andy; 'e knows 'ow to make 'is weapons, knows w'ot is good to eat and 'ow to get it. And 'e's ruddy well satisfied with w'ot 'e's got becos 'e don't know w'ot 'e's missing. We *do*. Twiggo? A savage used to cross a river on a log, syme way we did, astride of it, paddling with 'is 'ands. One chap gets the idea of carving out a log to keep 'is legs dry, maybe 'e finds one that's 'ollow to begin with. 'E thinks 'e's a wonder. 'Ow about us? We know all about steamers with lifts and electric lights and powerful engines, music and fine grub. But we can't myke one. We can't even 'ollow out a log. We can't apply w'ot we know."

"We can apply some of it," said Brett. "I can't imagine knowledge being wasted. We know about leverage and the principle of the wheel. We are handicapped, of course. We have been set back in the stone age, apparently, but, if we discovered copper and some harder metal, or copper alone, we would advance immediately. It took a long time for the savage to evolve the bow and arrow, it won't take us so long.

"Toward the end of the stone age they discovered the use of the grindstone. We can apply that and make fair tools after a little. We can hollow out a canoe, with a stone adze or by burning with hot stones. We can build a house after a while. We've got to apply our powers systematically and concentratedly and we'll find our ability growing all the time.

"It is my idea that one or two of us should concentrate on the manufacture of cloth and string, experimenting with pounded bark of various trees for the one and different fibers for the other. Some will have to supply the food and haul wood, some one else can tackle the tool problem, or the housing. We've got to get a settled mode of living in a simple way before we can go ahead to conveniences. Necessities first; then comforts. And we ought to get an idea of what sort of place we have landed on."

"And you bossing the outfit?"

"There will be no occasion for any boss that I can see, Malone. We're all equal here, as well as men can be. Some of us may turn out to be more useful to the general community than the rest but that would be a hard matter to decide. Any attempt at socialism is ridiculous. We each need the other's efforts for the mutual ability to live in any degree of comfort. If any man is sick and unable to do his share the rest will look out for him. If there is any law between us it must be that of unselfishness."

"And," suggested Tully, "if any man is well and *won't* do his share, you can place a bet with yourself that he won't get his share of what the others accomplish."

"Meanin' that for me?" snapped Malone. "I'll tell you one thing, my young sprig, I don't need the help of you mollycoddles for me to get by. Wolf and me could go it on our own and very nicely. Remember that."

"Walker found this cave; he got the eels."

"And I brought in most of the wood."

They were all on edge with the weather, the barometric depression, the lack of food. The fuel was down to the last stick, there was a half-ration of illy cooked, greasy eels. And they were acting more like children than men. Brett fought his own irritation.

"We should form a Committee of the Whole, I think," he suggested. "It would be a Ways and Means Committee. Each member would make his suggestions and we'll talk them over. Then we'll split into sub-committees with those who show the most aptitude for certain jobs in charge. Report progress at the evening campfire, discuss the next day's work. No need for even a chairman, or we can take that job in turn. Majority to rule." Malone grunted.

"No one likely to vote with me," he objected. "Wolf's plain dummy till he comes out of his trance. I suppose I get all the dirty work by the rule of the majority."

"Figuring you're always going to disagree with us, Malone?" Brett went on without a reply. "I fancy Walker and Tully know more about practical camp layout than any of us. Drainage, site, latrines, garbage. As for kitchen-police duty, we can all take regular turns at that—except Professor Harland." Harland promptly put in a protest overruled even by Malone.

"You spin us the yarns, prof," he said; "That's where you shine over any of us—unless O'Neill wants to show us how good he can act."

With the rest, O'Neill realized that Malone, conscious of his physical superiority to any of them, save Wolf and Wallaby Brown, was inclined to push that forward to the point of quarreling, as an offset to any mental deficiency he might feel on the social side.

"Go on, Brett," said Bowman. "You are elected chairman for this first meeting, anyway. Cont'ry minded, say no."

Brett strove to put enthusiasm into the council. Once started, the ball rolled well. Suggestions begat suggestions. Committees were formed, seemingly to everyone's satisfaction. There were to be no chairmen. On Sanitation: Tully and Walker. Provender Supplies: Walker, Bowman, O'Neill Brown, and Brett. Clothing: Walker, Bowman, Harland and O'Neill. Fuel: Tully, Wolf, Brown and Malone. Entertainment: Bowman, Harland and O'Neill. Building: Tully, Wolf, Brown, Malone and Brett. Weapons and Tools: Tully, Harland, Brown, Malone and Brett. Exploration: Walker, Bowman, O'Neill, Malone, Brett.

With the exception of Wolf, whose initiative was dormant but who appeared willing enough to do what tasks were suggested to him—and the professor, named for the less arduous tasks by reason of his age—every one was on four committees and it was agreed that they should give equal portions of their time to each unless it was agreed upon to increase that time on the matters most vital.

As for time, the shortest shadow every day marked noon. The professor suggested the securing of a container that could be regulated so that the water it held could drip through an aperture in exactly twenty-four hours. Once that was established, if the container was at all symmetrical, it could be marked off to represent the hours. "A water-clock, or clepsydra," he explained. "The ancients had the clepsydra so arranged that it played flutes during the night when the registration could not be observed. I don't know how the flutes could be managed."

"Where are you going to get your symmetrical container?" challenged Tully.

"That will be up to your Weapons and Tools Committee," retorted the professor and there was a hint of humor in his voice. "I suppose you expect to try your hand at clay bowls and pitchers and cooking pots."

"Never thought of it," said Brett. "But we surely will. As for the sunny hours, I should think we could register them with some sort of a sundial, scratched on stone. It depends, I believe, upon the angle of the gnomon-pointer. Its edge has to be parallel with the earth's axis. I happen to know that because we once bought a good-looking sundial in an antique store and then discovered that it was angled for Maine instead of California. I don't suppose we'll ever get one that's accurate. At the equator the gnomon would be almost flat. But we'll fudge out some sort of a time-clock."

Interest began to dwindle as the fire died down and their wounds and bruises began to reassert themselves. They had been forced to haul up the ladder log for fuel. Soaked as it was, it burned badly, giving off little or no warmth, requiring constant coaxing by blowing to do more than smolder.

The heavy rain seemed to act as a curtain, preventing egress of the smoke and the ventilation of the cave was none too good. Silence conquered all of them and, after a while, they huddled together forlornly in the ferns, all their plans balked by the dreary environment.

Sleep denied itself to Brett and he applied himself to the fire but the last log would only char sullenly and the glowing embers slowly changed to ash. It was pitchy black without, the same within. They could no longer see the rain but the sloshing, driving sound of it kept on, like a steady hammering on the armor of their valor.

Nature, he thought, was cruel, not beneficent. The Back to Nature cult were only pretenders, knowing nothing of true exposure. Man lived only by constant, strenuous endeavor. He protected himself by artificialities and the forces of Nature waged a steady warfare, a persistent pressure against civilization, angry at the wresting of some of its secrets, the victory over a part of its control.

Nature was a treacherous and unsleeping foe. Man existed in comfort only by improving upon her, by building a world within the world, by the utmost use of his wit and invention. Ultimately the earth would grow cold, man, despite his most desperate efforts, his research in chemistry, his production of light and heat and force and food, his artificial dwellings, must succumb. Then the vegetable kingdom would disappear, the highest forms of life dying first and, in the end, the mineral kingdom alone would exist of the three, as it was in the beginning. Mother Nature would reign in Chaos.

He combated this waking nightmare. They were men and they could fight. Once the rain ceased. He drowsed off at last to the remorseless pelt of it but not before he had summoned the forces of his reason, rallied them, convinced himself that in him was a spark of life that was more than elementary, that was greater in its essence than the manifestations known as Nature, that furnished, not only the will to triumph over conditions, but the power.

The night, if it was night, changed insensibly to day. They woke cold and hungry, tried in vain to sleep again and, at last, saw a lightening of the spaces back of the rain, sensed a lessening of the downpour. Dimly the interior of the cave became visible, farther and farther in. It was easier to breathe. The rain changed swiftly to an ordinary storm, then to a drizzle, and finally ceased.

They could see the opposing cliffs and the woods, green once more. The gray clouds, woolly masses driving fast, began to break up, a patch of blue showed, widening rapidly. Birds began to call. A golden, blessed shaft of sunshine struck down the canyon. The gray clouds were now pearly white. The world took on color, warmth. By the sun it seemed a little after noon. Great areas of wood and rocks and earth glowed brightly. Vapors began to mount, sucked up from the sodden soil, but the sun lorded it over all.

The river was now a swirling flood, dun colored. The waterfall was diminished to half its height but enormously swollen in volume. Uprooted trees went swirling down midstream or rode in eddies. Many of them would be stranded, there would be no lack of wood.

The sunshine beat on the threshold of the cavern and they basked in it, surveying their changed world, reveling in the heat before they attempted to descend. Wolf, naked, lolled his hairy body on the ledge, first on his back and then on his belly. Bowman began to whistle a jazz tune. Tully joined in. Brett felt vigor flooding him. His aches vanished; his hunger dulled its edge. The professor quoted——

The Eye of Phoebus, brazen but benign.

Malone rolled a complacent eye toward him. To the oiler the professor spoke a language that was hard to follow sometimes, yet the chip-on-the-shoulder attitude Malone exhibited toward the rest vanished in all his contacts with the scholar, toward whom he showed admiration and a measure of protection.

"Sure," he said, "sure thing, prof!"

The glory of the sun grew stronger. Presently they would be shrinking again from its aggressive rays, smashing through their tender skin. Now they reveled in them. The mists grew along the slopes of the hills.

From their cave aerie they could see above the waterfall, but the vapors denied them all save glimpses of a swollen river bordered by trees. The air shook with the rumble of the waterfall, the sub-tone of the current seaward. Now and then a log came over the fall, lifting, tilting, diving.

As they watched they saw a whitish object washed down and over in the brown flood, an object that struggled and seemed to be alive. It plunged into the pool, submerged and came up, a living thing that struck the water with its limbs and squealed as it swam, squealed hideously with a strangely familiar cry that made them all look sharply at each other, blinking with surprise, then gaze again at the river where the thing was swimming in a circle.

"For the love of Pete, it's a pig!" Tully leaned forward in his excitement as he shouted and nearly fell off the ledge. Brett swung off, hung by his finger-ends and dropped, calling up to O'Neill as the most available ally. "Come on, we've got to get it."

O'Neill lit beside him and they ran down the slippery slope to the pool. Back of them the rest, save the professor, too stiff and weak to attempt the unassisted jump, landed and followed them, excited as a lot of schoolboys, shouting as they ran while the pig squealed its terror.

Brett remembered a saying that a swimming pig cut its throat with its sharp hoofs when it swam, but this creature seemed in no danger of such suicide. It progressed lustily enough, lacking only either sense of direction or force enough of stroke to guide it out of the eddy that swung it round the basin that now was brimful. The natural exit was partly blocked by entangled trees, their boughs locked like the horns of fighting deer, their matted roots offering a resting place for the porker, though with only opportunity to lodge its fore feet.

It was a young pig, white of body, curly of tail and pink of mouth. It was a sacrificial pig upon the altar of Opportunity. It was the first piece of real luck they had come across. And the sight of it made them ravenous where they had been merely hungry. As an apple arouses the secretions of the schoolboy's salivary glands so, a hundred times more, did the pig summon all the emotions of appetite, colored by imagination and memory. They had been moving perilously along the arc that is marked with the two goals, life and death, moving far too close to the gradation labeled starvation.

Now the pendulum swung swiftly in the opposite direction. Naked men, racing down a water-ravaged slope intent upon their kill of living meat, with only hands for weapons. They were obsessed with but one emotion—hunger—and they made for their prey with the merciless intent of the famished tiger—without his facilities for butchery.

The little pig saw them coming and knew their mood, knew these weird beings that ran and leaped on their long hind legs boded him no good. He was nearly done up with his struggle against the water that had caught him asleep on an undermined bank, with his dive over the fall. He was too weak and too scared to do anything but hang on with his fore-hoofs and rend the air with his useless clamor. Brett and O'Neill dived in together and swam for the trees. Walker shouted after them:

"Don't drown 'im. Bring 'im alive. If you drown 'im 'e won't bleed."

"How about a fire?" demanded Tully. "I'm hungry enough but I can't stomach raw pork. The fire's out and all the wood's soaking, anyway."

"How about this stuff?" Bowman pointed to a great trunk that had stranded near to them. It was that of a tree attacked by blight, perhaps partly destroyed by lightning. One half of it was dead, paralyzed. The bark had shrunk away from a decayed split, like a wound. A jagged rock had caught in the split, rent the bark. It was thick and it showed inner layers of fine tissue, not unlike a birch though the outer skin was very different.

"Strip off the rest of that bark and I bet you'll find kindling," said Bowman. "You brought over some of those flints, Malone, didn't you? Let's all take a whack at starting a fire."

Brett's suggestion of fracturing the flinty dike by fire and water had been carried out by Malone successfully and he had taken the most likely looking fragments to the cave before the storm broke. The obsidian had ruptured conchoidally with concave depressions and convex elevations surrounded by more or less jagged and thin edges, sharp enough but pre-senting the difficulties of a badly hacked blade. Some of these curving surfaces comfortably fitted the palm, forming a species of handle for the broken margin. Others suggested heads for weapons, from slivers for ar-rows to jagged pieces that, bound in cleft or forked sticks, would make effective tomahawks or clubs.

Malone ran back to the cave and the professor threw down to him the broken flints. Tully, Bowman, Brown, Walker and Malone started searching for stones that looked likely contacts for sparks, testing them, tossing them away, all feverishly striving to conjure the precious element out of the rocks as Moses once brought water. Wolf, balked by the flood, stood on the verge of it watching the chase.

Had it not been of such deadly earnest to all of them the triangular water combat would have been ludicrous as the chasing of a greased pig at a fair. O'Neill and Brett both grabbed a hind leg at the same moment and drew the pig under water. Its frenzied kicks forced them to let go after all three had submerged. The frightened brute snapped at them, gulped water, went under and emerged again while they tried to get a grip on it that would let them tow it to land. Brett appraised Walker's advice as good. Drowned pig would be apt to have its blood coagulated.

At last the porker found some lodgment on a boulder in shallower water. Chasing it closely, the swimmers touched bottom, flung themselves on their quarry and floundered ashore with it squawking and struggling frantically. It got clear, leaving O'Neill with a split chin from a blow of its cloven hoof. With a last desperate burst of strength it scurried for cover. Wolf, yelling, bounded after, overtook it, lunged for a leg and got it. Shifting grip he whirled the porker aloft by both hind legs and brought its head smashing against a rock. Walker came running with a jagged flint and hacked at its throat.

It was murder, bloody and barbarous, that they committed. The reek of the rich red blood in the hot sun, the crude disembowelment, the smoking entrails, the hacked disjointing! At other times it would have been nauseating, but the savage was to the front in all of them.

Bowman had found a free-sparking combination. Tully divided the inner laminations of the bark and found that it was dry and gave out a fragrant balsam. He pounded some of it into pulp and placed this in a recess between rocks as Brett had done. As Bowman sent out a shower of sparks Tully blew on the fibrous stuff and got smoke, then fire. The flame, pale in the sun, licked freely at the fuel and it burned with sudden bursts. Brown tore off great chunks of outer bark, snapped off the smaller boughs where the sap had gone out of the tree, broke fragments across his knee. As the fire steadily grew they lugged over a small tree that had been deposited by the flood which was now rapidly retreating, carried off by the river channel.

The blaze became a furnace. The butchers, spotted with blood all over, smeared with it up to the elbows, brought over their ill-shaped joints. Two forked branches were set up, a slender but tough limb was peeled with a flint, thrust skewer-wise through the severed loin and placed across the prongs. Had the fire died to ashes their cookery would have been better but they could not wait and the red and yellow tongues coiled about the meat as the fat dripped down and sputtered explosively. The hairy hide protected the meat in some measure. Walker, as chief cook, turned his spit, gradually they got a bed of ashes and the savor of the food set them a-slavering.

Malone went to the cave with a new ladder-tree. Wolf helped him carry it. Whether from close association in the fire-room and consequent ease and some measure of trust, only Malone out of all of them could get Wolf to do his simple share of the work. The ladder was for the professor, taken under Malone's wing.

"Come on, prof," he cried. "Pork tenderloin cooked to a turn. Sure. the cracklin's a bit fuzzy but the meat smells like heaven."

The professor came down a little reluctantly, assisted by Malone. He was inclined to shrink from Wolf. He had seen the brutal ease and strength with which the oiler had swung up the pig and smashed its skull against the rock. Appetite fought with mental nausea and won.

Salt they had none. They had not needed it with the shellfish nor missed it with the fish that Walker had caught. It was only as they became filled with the meat that they realized what was lacking. They ate like cavemen, tearing the cooked flesh apart with their greasy fingers, sucking them afterward, flinging aside the hairy hide with its scorched bristles.

With full stomachs they sought shade where they could find it and slept as if they had been drugged. When they awoke, the carcass of the pig was in a fair way to be wasted, spoiled, alive with buzzing flies in the hot sun. They surveyed it ruefully. To preserve meat in that temperature was another problem they had to face. They managed to separate both legs where the hide had prevented the flies from blowing. These they cooked for supper. The rest of the pig they buried with the entrails, scooping out a pit in the sand for the purpose, scattering sand over the blood.

"Next time we get a pig we'll cook the whole carcass in your underground oven on hot stones, Wallaby," said Brett. "It is up to the Supplies

Committee to get us that pig. There must be a herd of them. Probably that was what the beasts were hunting the other night."

"Or the wild hogs were hunting them. A wild boar is no joke, I imagine," said Bowman. "If we can find their runways we could dig pitfalls and cover them with sheets of bark and dirt on top of that. You couldn't get them with a deadfall. Wonder what they eat? If it's roots they may be good for us."

"Truffles, for instance," suggested Tully ironically.

"There might be yams, or peanuts. Then—I've seen 'em pickle hams and smoke them many a time. We could build a smoke house easy enough."

"Sure," said Malone. "All you need is an ax to cut down some trees, a saw to make planks with, a hammer and a pound o' nails. Easy."

Bowman flashed him a look of scorn. "You get me a pig, Malone, and I'll fix up the smoke house. I'll make it out of bricks if I have to, or weave the walls like sheep hurdles and plaster them with clay." Malone subsided. Brett swallowed a chuckle. Tully and Bowman were coming to the front. At the beginning Walker had seemed to possess the initiative and it had piqued him a little to find the younger Americans slow to start. But they were getting their stride. Walker smacked his lips unctuously.

"Broiled 'am!" he exclaimed rapturously. "But no eggs, unless I make me a suit of wickerwork armor to fool those birds."

"Meantime," Brett suggested, "the fat we've cooked is going to help us against sunburn. It won't smell pleasant but I'm not so fussy as I was." He surveyed his body, scratched, blistered, stained and swollen and ran his fingers through his stubble of beard. "I'm going to clean up a bit. I look like a Digger Indian and I begin to feel like one." It wouldn't be hard for a man to slide to the bottom of the social scale in such circumstances, he reflected. That was one thing they had to guard against, the lack of such civilizing things as razors and shears, brushes and combs, towels and handkerchiefs.

Malone and Wolf made no ablutions. They laughed at the rest, trying to get clean without soap, in cold water. Tully, drying off, fingered a clayey bank. "We ought to be able to make pots and bowls out of this. It's fine. The sun would bake it or we might make a little kiln after we'd made bricks and sunbaked them for Bowman's smoke-house. We could heat water and boil our food."

"Would they hold water, unglazed?"

"Seems to me I've read that salt will give a glaze. We've got to make salt. That's simple enough."

"And up in Maine they still make their own soft-soap. Pour water through wood ashes and boil it up with fried-out fat and grease. They salt it out with brine to make hard soap."

"Good for you, Tully!" Brett's eyes brightened as he nodded at him. The knowledge stored haphazard in their brains was cropping out in the right time and place with the proper association of ideas. In one way they were enormously above the savage; they knew what could be done. Once protected against the first tests of Nature as to their fitness to exist and he began to think they would shortly be able to establish themselves with a fair degree of comfort. There was a zest to the contest that began to enter into it.

The absorbing earth, the water-shedding surfaces, the vaporizing sun, combined with the natural flow of the river and the ebb of the tide to reduce rapidly the flooded area. They resolved to spend the night in the cave and make their first organized start in the morning. Toward evening mosquitoes rose in swarms and drove them back of their fire, seated in the smudge.

The pork-grease they had smeared on their skins helped to protect them against the wandering squadrons that found them out and also acted as an emollient for their sun-scald and bird-bites. Wherever the skin was broken there seemed to be a disposition to fester. The tropic climate appeared to breed a surplus of bacilli, eager to enter through the slightest breach in man's armor and destroy him as the creepers and other parasites choked the trees. For their susceptible white man's tissues clothing was a paramount necessity.

Yet they slept. There was no Aeneid that night. Slumber seized and bound them fast. Once Brett awoke and heard howling and snarling. He looked out. The sky was cloudy, an aftermath of the storm, the light uncertain. The moon struggled through its vaporous veils and showed him a number of great beasts swarming where they had buried the remains of the pig. He was still heavy with sleep and he went back to his ferns secure in the knowledge that their cave was a citadel. He woke for the second time just after dawn and lay in the half light dozing.

As the light strengthened slowly and the rest still lay unconscious of time and place, Brett began to weave a vision of the future. In it were included cultivated fields, domesticated hogs, orchards of selected trees, rows of berry-fruits, even lawns and flower-beds about a low bungalow, with brick sides, perhaps, and a cozy thatched roof, with wide porches where men lounged after the pleasant, healthful labor of the day.

Why not? It was all practical. They could learn to do all this. As for furniture, blind men could make wicker chairs and couches. If Brett had been a man with a home he would—this he had often told himself, feeling the itch for such matters—have been a house-tinkerer and amateur gardener. Some were born with the desire and the knack of handling tools and making things grow. A measure of creative instinct. To bring order out of the wilderness, to bend Nature to his purpose, to build up a little civilization of their own seemed to him a thing well worth achieving. Something in his vitality responded to the call—not of the wild—but its redemption.

A yawn that changed to a sigh aroused him. O'Neill was hunched up gazing toward the cave entrance where a gull sailed by, slanted, peered in and soared on.

"Look at that beggar," said O'Neill as Brett stirred. "Free as the air and we cooped up. Brett, how are we going to get off this —— place and get back home?"

Brett shrugged his shoulders. The prospect appeared infinitely remote, infinitesimal. He could sympathize with O'Neill, cut off from all that made life pleasant, success, adulation, luxury. Yet he felt that he could get along without it.

"You might call in at the steamer office and get a time table, O'Neill," said Walker. "And, while you're down town, buy me a package of baccy and a pipe. Wake up, man. You're on the Supplies Committee. If you don't want cold pig for breakfast we'd better get busy foraging for food. How about berries and some oysters, or would you rather 'ave a chilled grapefruit, oatmeal and cream, corfee and eggs Benedict? Shall I serve you in your state-room, sir?"

O'Neill frowned. Then he laughed. "You go to blazes," he said. "Just now I'd swap all the oysters in the world, pearls included, for a nice new toothbrush."

106 / J. ALLAN DUNN

"Try the end of a chewed stick," said Tully. "Trouble with you is you've been pampered. You'll be growling for a clean suit of B. V. D.'s next thing."

It was good-humored chaff. And O'Neill was getting more human, Brett decided, as, with Bowman and Brown, the Supplies Committee sallied forth into the rose and pearl of a perfect morning. Laughter was a great leaven. Walker broke into one of his ditties as they walked down toward the river, now down to nearly normal:

> *Oh, 'e used to grind a corfee mill.*
> *And 'e mixed the sugar with the sand.*
> *At the pub around the corner w'en the shop was closed*
> *The drinks all round 'e'd stand. Well—'e grinds a diff'rent mill just now*
> *And 'e breaks a lot of stone.*
> *And all becos the pore boy mixed*
> *'Is marster's money with 'is own.*

CHAPTER VII.
PROGRESS.

WORK STARTED with vim. Walker went off to fish, O'Neill to gather salt and make evaporation pools. Professor Harland determined to experiment with the production of string and of weaves for hats, for mats and for the many purposes to which it might be put. The string problem was a vital one to solve. It meant nets, the binding of flints to wood for tools and weapons, the tying together of lumber for building purposes. Harland had the patience; his long fingers promised dexterity. Grass, stringy bark fibers and fern ribs were the materials he proposed to practice upon.

Malone and Wolf got in a wood supply. Brett took Tully with him to try to find a camp-site that would be above the possibility of flood-reach. He hoped to find a grassy plateau with some shade and a living spring, with good soil, not far from timber supply. The cave had manifest disadvantages of which lack of ventilation and the stench of the bat droppings were the worst but far from the only ones. Brett had in mind a house on stilts for security.

If he could find four trees making up a fair rectangle of the right dimensions he figured on using these for his corner posts. If he was fortunate enough he might find boughs angling out on all four at approximately the same height. In these crotches they could place crosspoles for the frame, fastening them with creepers or hand-made rope. Then the platform of split saplings—they could use stone wedges for that work—a thick carpet of ferns, plaited sides of wide grasses or long leaves, a thatch of grass, overhanging to shed the rain, and they would have a tree home, reached by ladders, a nest that would be shady, always tolerably cool, for rest and sleep.

All his requirements might not be forthcoming, but he went out with Tully to see what he could see.

Bowman was full of plans for a fish weir that sounded eminently practical, if they could evolve a net. If not, he had suggestions for traps to be made of wicker; cylinders several feet in length and three or more in diameter with funnel-like entrances, on the principle of a safety inkwell, through which the fish might pass to the bait or be carried by the force of the current, finding themselves unable to discover the small exit.

"The main thing is the weir," he explained to Brown, his assistant engineer. "We'll pick a place downstream below a stretch of deep water. If we can find a bar for foundation so much the better, as long as it is likely to be permanent. We'll build a wall with stones halfway across the river so that fish can cross it at high tide but at low the top of it will be out of water or near enough so as to make it too shallow for them to pass.

"Then we'll make the weir of upright sticks stuck close together to make a tight fence for the other half of the stream. We can bind these together with the same creepers Brett used on the raft. Where the current is strongest we leave a gap. The whole thing is a sort of trap, half of it wide open at flood water which, I figure, is the time a lot of the fish come up river. They'll come in and feed—soon as the tide turns and drops enough toward the top of our wall, we close the gap with the net.

"The fish find the water lowering or getting less salty and they start down current into the bag. It's the only way they can get out. Upstream we'll have the waterfall to block 'em, if that's necessary. But I imagine most of the fish that come up with the tide'll try all they know to get back with it. Anyway we'll see."

"Some plan," said Wallaby. "I wouldn't think of that in a million years. I've got a one-cylinder brain; that's one big reason why I didn't come away with the championship. I could hit as 'ard as the other fellows, maybe 'arder. I could stand the gaff as much and I was willing to mix it, but you Yanks think quicker. I don't think much, not to really sit down and work things out like you and Brett and young Tully. O'Neill's smart enough, too, only he'd rather 'ave the other fellow do it. Gen'ally 'ad things that way. And the prof, his brains are different. Sort of storage plant."

"How about Malone?" asked Bowman as they went slowly down stream, looking for the likely place for their dam and weir as well as for materials.

"Malone 'ates everyone who 'e thinks is apt to think that 'e's a cut above Malone. Savvy what I mean? Sore at the world. Most stokers are. Specially on ship. They sweat and broil at their mucky backbreaking job, drying up while they chuck coal, an' w'en they crawl up on deck for a breath of cool, fresh air, wet an' grimy an' stiff, they get a peek at the first-class passengers all dressed up in whites, stretched out on long chairs, with a long glass with ice and a stick in it an' they cuss 'em out. Looks to them like white to black, the difference between 'em.

"You carnt 'ardly blame 'em. And it gets into their system. Malone, 'e's allus figured 'e was just as good a man as anyone—better if it came down to muscles. On'y 'e'd never 'ad a square show. Now 'e's landed 'ere with the same chance as the rest an' 'ere's Walker smarter than 'e is; 'ere's Brett making 'im look like a monkey; 'ere's the prof gyme as they make 'em an' full of savvy; 'ere's you with this fish-trap an' Tully thinking out pots and pans and soap.

"Where does Malone come in? 'E can carry wood. Back in 'is 'ead 'e knows 'e ain't making much of a showing, that 'e ain't as smart as the rest of you but it just makes 'im sore. 'E still pats 'imself on the back and tells 'imself 'e can lick you. Still the better man."

"How about Wolf—and you?"

"Wolf's 'is pal, in a way. Same grade. Malone jolly well knows I can lick 'im, so 'e leaves me alone. Then he's cut off from 'is booze and baccy an' *that* makes 'im sore. More than the rest of us who use it. Why? Becos this is the first time in years Malone's ever been ashore and sober. By and by 'e'll clear up, I wouldn't wonder. How about these for your poles?"

Bowman inspected them.

"Look like dogwood," he said. "Fine, if we can manage to cut them."

The trees, slim-trunked, grew in swampy ground. Brown found it possible to pull some of them up by main strength, roots and all, but this did not furnish them with any driving point. Hacking at them with the flints they had brought was a botchy process.

"Let's choose our place and get ahead with the wall," said Bowman. "We can tote the poles back and burn them in the fire. We can scrape off the char better than we can trim the wood and burning will harden them." Brown nodded recognition of the wisdom and they waded out into the stream to decide upon their location. Noon found them hard at it piling stones when a call from camp summoned them. There were berries, broiled fish-with-salt and Walker, as chef, produced triumphantly from the ashes some brown tubers that looked like enlarged sweet potatoes, some of them jointed, two feet in length.

"Sir Walter Raleigh discovered potaters," said Walker. "Sir Tyrone O'Neill discovers yams. Try 'em. They ain't over and above mealy; they'd be better with butter an' pepper, but they ain't 'arf bad with salt."

He split open one of the bulbous roots disclosing reddish, waxy pulp.

"They'll have starch in them," said the professor. "I imagine we need that to offset our meat diet."

"An Irishman, potaters an' pigs go together. O'Neill found where the pigs 'ad been grubbing them up. Now we can dig those pits and get some pork. We ought to 'ave kept some of that hide for leather, guv'nor. My sneakers are beginnin' to go to pieces and 'ow you folks get along without any shoes is beyond me."

"We keep off rocks," said Brett, addressed as "guv'nor" by the steward. "Pigskin would be hard for us to handle. But the shoe problem has got to be taken up. Sharkskin might work if we could tan and soften it."

"Who catches the sharks?" inquired Walker. "Not me."

The little jest got a laugh. Laughs were beginning to come more readily and they rounded off the corners of scarcity and drudgery. Wolf, gobbling, stuffing himself, remained apathetic. Hunkered down where the others sat on rocks or logs, his long arms covered with hair, his matted chest and bearded face gave him the appearance of a great ape that had never achieved speech or laughter. But he worked well.

After the meal Bowman and Brown hurried back to their dam; Tully took Walker off to the camp sites that he and Brett had thought possible. Brett walked over to the pile of wood that Malone and Wolf were assembling. The professor went down to the stream where he was trying his plaiting under water, as Panama hat-weaves are said to be made, and where he had some bark-string fibers soaking. O'Neill went with him.

Brett's mind was fixed on sandals. Until they could make some survey of the place he felt uneasy. To climb the crater was obviously the best method and to attempt to pass over the lava without some protection for foot soles was predetermined failure. He thought that he might—pending the manufacture of leather—utilize bark. He had sharpened three of the nails from the boat to chisel-edges on a stone—Walker had four more in use as hooks, the rest Brett reserved to use as awls.

There were many varieties of trees in the pile, more still scattered along flood edge. Above the waterfall he fancied there might even be a small jam. He examined the various barks, testing them with his chisel, trying to select one that would be tough and fairly elastic. The nails were clumsy tools, not long enough to give him a good grip, and he found difficulty in handling them until he thought of heating one and boring a hole in a bit of hardwood, using this as a socket in which to insert the head end of the nail, hammering it farther in with a stone and rewhetting. He was as proud of the result as a boy with his first pocket knife—prouder, with the glow of the inventor.

Now he could sample the bark with fair facility but the first real discovery he made was not in connection with his sandals. He cut into a soft tree-skin and found underneath inner layers that were white and papery, far more so than the stuff they had used the night before for kindling. Of the species of the tree he knew nothing but he was beginning to find his editorial reading coming into play.

Tapa cloth, he had read a score of times, in South Sea literature, was made from such inner bark, steeped and then pounded with a wooden club until it widened as it became thinner. Strips could be pounded together until the soft tissues welded. If this material could be so used the clothing question was partly disposed of, so far as covering and protection from insects and sunburn was concerned. He shouted to O'Neill and the actor came running.

Brett explained to him what he knew—or thought he knew—of the manufacture of tapa cloth and O'Neill, taking a chisel, set to work tearing off the outer bark and securing the papery strips for experimentation while Brett went on with his search for a leather substitute.

He found bark at last that looked as if it might do and managed to carve two sections into shapes an inch or two greater than the scratched outline of his foot. Using the rounded edge of a boulder he contrived to hammer the edges so that they turned up and found that the tough fibers held well together. He relieved O'Neill of the soft leather belt and cut most of it up into long narrow thongs with his nail-tool, returning O'Neill the remainder.

He bored clean holes through the bark with a heated nail and laced his thongs over his insteps and about his heels. He could walk without shuffling. He had made a good job of it though the sandals shifted a little. But the relief to his feet was great, he no longer had to pick his path gingerly. He trotted a short distance in his elation. How long the bark would last was doubtful, but the supply was pretty sure to be plentiful, the trouble of making up half a dozen pairs for a day's trip amounted to nothing.

He showed them to O'Neill and the professor. Malone came up to inspect them and even Wolf let out a grunt that tokened approval. They dropped their work and started in as shoemakers. There were eight thongs. One sufficed for each sandal. But the professor was confident he could weave together fiber string before sundown and they could always plait strips of cloth from their travesties of garments, now stained and torn almost beyond the utility point as to the pajamas. And Walker had the laces of his shoes. As yet the shoes themselves were better than sandals. Brett cut out an extra pair of soles for Tully and left for the camp site. O'Neill contracted to provide for Bowman and Brown. It was an eventful day of real achievement and progress, coupled with the inspiration of their own growing prowess.

The place they determined on for their house-building was on a grassy terrace well above the river, jutting out from the main escarpment of the cliff and set here and there with trees. Unable to find four as conveniently placed as their wishes had planned they finally discovered two with forking boughs about fifteen feet up and almost on the same level. And there were convenient rifts in the cliff, which would form the back wall of their tree-dwelling, into which the ends of cross poles might be thrust and plugged secure. The resulting frame would not be exactly rectangular but they were not particular and they could get a level floor.

Out of a larger cleft in the precipice a little stream was flowing. This ravine, fern set, was wide enough for exploration and Brett determined that the source of the water was from veins in the cliff and not the afterseepage of the storm. It came out freely, clear and sparkling, and its tiny course was well marked with smooth water-worn stones that established it as a fairly permanent supply.

As with Bowman and Brown, their main obstacle was the felling of trees. The uneven edges of the flint fragments promised a sorry exchange for ax or hatchet. The boughs of the trees uprooted by the flood might be burned off, Brett considered, if they could find enough of them the right shape. They left that difficulty for later, contenting themselves with choosing a place for their cooking, and for the latrine. Rapidly lengthening shadows sent them back to the cave where they found the rest already assembled and supper preparing.

The dam was nearly completed; they all had footgear of a sort; O'Neill produced some dried out stretches of papery cloth and Professor Harland exhibited several lengths of string, somewhat clumsily spliced but promising a supply of cordage with practice. It was a banner day.

The sun sank behind the cliff, dark night fell like a curtain and they sat by their fire, tired but self congratulatory, united by common labor and success, laying out the next day's achievements. By universal consent the Exploration Committee was extended to the whole of the party. Fish, yams and berries were easy to procure. No one wanted to be left behind and it was a measure of safety for them to go together on a long trip. They might run across the beasts that howled in the night; there was still the possibility of natives.

"Are you too tired, professor," asked Malone, "to spin us some more of that yarn? I'm wanting to know what happened and unless I get something to make me forget the craving for a smoke I'll not sleep tonight."

"I shall be glad, to do that." So, for an hour, Professor Harland recited the rhythmic lines he had translated and kept fresh in his memory for the love of their beauty and the stirring tale they told. It seemed almost as if he was setting forth their own adventure at times:

Brightly sparkled the sea in the tremulous glory of moonlight.
Soon they were cautiously skirting the shores of the Island of Circe,
Where with unending song the Sun's luxurious daughter
Thrilled the desolate groves, and in her imperial palace
Conquered the darkness of night by the glare of sweet torches of cedar,
Flashing through daintiest warp the woof of her rhythmical shuttle.
Thence was plainly heard the furious growling of lions
Quarreling with their chains and filling the night with their roaring:
There, too, bears and bristly boars in strong-fenced enclosures
Grunted and snarled, and monstrous wolves were incessantly howling:
Whom by her potent herbs had Circe divine without mercy
Changed from the likeness of men to grim-visaged beasts of the forest.

Harland stopped to clear his throat and in the silence, far off, echoing against unseen cliffs, they heard the howling of the hunting pack starting out on their nightly raid. It was even more eerie than before, safe though they were in the cave, coming pat as it did upon Virgil's colorful description. They sat hearkening with the same grisly feeling of ghost-hairs rising on their spines.

"I'd like it better if they were in strong-fenced enclosures," said Bowman in a whisper. "First thing tomorrow I'm going to make me a club and a spear. Fits right in, don't it?"

"Barring the lady who played witch with 'em."

"That happened a long time ago, Malone," said Walker. "Go on, professor."

"Maybe it did," countered Malone. "But there's a lot of men haven't got over the spell yet. And I'd take the chance of it, at that, if she was good lookin'. Faith, I'd be willing to do a good deal to lay eyes on a pretty girl."

"I'm coming to one in a minute," said the professor dryly and went on to Lavinia, daughter of Latinus.

Ripe already for love and dreaming already of marriage.

Lavinia, who was to bring about another Trojan war and the bloody rivalry of Aeneas and Turnus. He stopped with the end of the seventh book, the gathering of the clans for war. They saw the kindling fires, they heard the brazen call of trumpets, they beheld the horsemen and the chariots, the champing steeds, the flashing armor, the tribesmen rallying for the fight. And, by the power of the dead poet and the force of language, they forgot the island, forgot their own plight and listened spellbound in a witchery as strong as that of Circe with her golden rod, a witchery that entered presently into their dreams.

CHAPTER VIII.
THE PACK.

THE PROFESSOR awoke slightly feverish, threatened with an attack of what might develop into dysentery. He made no complaint beyond the fact that he would rather remain in the cave as he did not feel up to the exploration party, but Brett got him to declare his symptoms and felt the fevered head and hands with some alarm. His knowledge of medicines and sickness was slight. So was that of the rest. With Brett, practice was confined to the administration of ordinary well-known remedies found in every family medicine-chest or obtained at the corner drugstore. Walker, Brown and Tully knew how to apply first aid, if they had a kit. Beyond doubt the woods harbored certain roots, herbs, barks, leaves, flowers and fruits that were sovereign remedies for many ailments; bonesets, astringents, febrifuges, purgatives, stimulants, but, unless they could recognize any of them—and this was doubtful—their efficacy could only be determined by hazardous experiment.

It was a wonder, he reflected, that sickness had not appeared before among them after their exposures and unusual diet. It was a warning, the first showing of a phantom that would ever stalk them. More of Nature's attacking forces—Sickness—Pestilence.

Some sort of pharmacoepia they must establish as soon as possible. As it was, they could handle surgery better than medicine. During the hours of securing breakfast, preparation and eating and the manufacture of crude weapons—spears, clubs and daggers—with flints or stones bound on to wood by the fiber twine, the professor dozed intermittently while one or the other tried to reduce the fever with cold compresses made by soaking O'Neill's paper cloth. Brett diagnosed the attack as malaria, carried by the mosquitoes. He foresaw that garbage and waste must be dealt with daily in the hot climate or they would be exposed to typhoid.

It was close to noon before they were in any shape to start. The professor insisted that he was much better and that the trip should not be put off on his account. His skin appeared moister and he had suffered no chills. He was able to sit up, though he did not care to eat. The pit-holes on the cave threshold, filled with water, would supply him. The cliff was in shadow for the rest of the day until the late afternoon and it would keep cool. Still Brett hesitated. Malone volunteered to stay. Tully suggested that they should draw lots in the matter but the protests of Harland grew so vigorous that they seemed likely to make him worse.

"You'll be back by sundown," he said. "I have fire and water and food if I need it. I'll sleep most of the time you are gone. I'm perfectly safe."

At the last moment Wolf balked on the trip. Malone, the only one with whom the Slovak would attempt to hold communication, reported that Wolf was bent on going fishing. Walker had had a monopoly of the sport and the oiler now demanded that he be allowed a chance.

"He's a stubborn cuss," said Malone. "'But he can keep an eye on the cave and if he catches anything it won't come amiss. I'll tell him he's got to keep the fire going. He says he don't give a hoot for scenery. He don't want to know what the place looks like. All he wants is to get away from it." Walker turned over his tackle and they left Wolf, showing more apparent interest than he had since they landed, casting his line with the current.

It was a hot afternoon though they did not notice it at first, making their way through the dense forest that covered the crater's flank. The trees were much like Brett's California redwoods and the ground was covered with the mold of rusted needles, soft and pleasant going where they carried their sandals, lacing them on again as they emerged on a twist of lava flow that had drawn a sharp line of demarcation between trees and the volcanic desert.

This burned-out slag was brown and porous. It lay in long twists like rope, or like giant loops and coils of pulled candy. Bowman suggested it resembled the entrails of some antediluvian monsters. In it grew cactus now in flower, promising, later on, prickly pears. Also plants like Spanish bayonet, or soapweed, save that the long leaves were unthorned and covered with long silvery hair.

Farther up the slope they encountered fine cinders that gave way to a powdery black dirt, sulfur-yellow beneath the weathered surface. Then came more of the candy lava, badly broken up by explosions or by the weather. Now and then one of them broke through the treacherous crust and scraped a leg against the sharp rim of the hole. There was worse ahead, dark gray lava resembling obsidian that had cooled, it seemed, in the very waves of its flow. Some of these petrified billows were ten feet from valley to crest, sharply pitched. The bark sandals saved the feet but not the ankles.

Lack of vessels in which to carry water soon made itself painfully manifest as they labored over these difficulties, persevering, with Brett in the lead, none willing to call a halt until he did. Their flimsy clothes were saturated with sweat that oozed continually out of them like water through an unglazed crock. The ferns with which they had shaded head and neck wilted. The rocks refracted the heat that poured down on them, doubled it.

There was no wind. Between storms, the breeze seemed only to blow after sunset. They struggled past the flinty stuff and got to smoother ground, plastered by the taffy-like lava that had flowed at a higher temperature. They began to make good progress, drawing close to the top of the crater and the mouth of its shaft. The all-important question as to whether they were marooned on an island or whether, by some blessed chance, they were on the mainland after all, urged them feverishly on to the summit. Brett held a secondary curiosity to examine the crater for signs of activity, or sulfur they could use in making matches, but the anxiety regarding their situation was paramount. Hope ebbed and flowed like a tide.

They suddenly found their way barred by a deep crack, extending diagonally. Some masses of rock gave welcome shadow. For the first time they faced the view.

They were on an island.

There was no doubt of it. The little dominion lay plain beneath them, green with vegetation that was splotched by the up-thrust of barren cliffs, red and black. The stream ran through their home ravine like a silver ribbon. To their right—and the east—was thick forest. Beyond it there was what appeared to be marsh with a small lake gleaming and another stream that flowed east and south to an almost circular bay, nearly as large as the one where they had landed and which they could plainly see between two sharp horns of cliff, one of which formed the northern cape of the island. The eastern part, beyond the marsh, was pinched into a narrow neck leading to a headland formed by a second crater, only a little smaller than the one on which they stood. There was a long pocket of a bay across the neck from the one into which the swamp river flowed. Off its entrance was an island, a cone similar to Bird Island which lay north and west.

The sea lay like *moiré* ribbon of deep blue, stretching to an illimitable horizon, hopeless of speck of land or sail to their straining eyes. Their island was just a tiny oasis in an ocean desert whose vast solitude numbed their souls.

The line of the barrier reef was plainly marked by a line of grayish white and by the sharp change in color inside the coral where the water was jade-green mottled by purple where the shallows rose. They could see the reef opening off Bird Island and a wider one at the circular harbor to the south. The forest stretched around the base of the crater to the south and spurred out, margining the swamp. Other dark woods backed the northern cape.

"Lonely enough," commented Bowman.

"How d'you suppose we ever came to hit it?"

"If this is the top of some submerged mountain range or lost continent," said Brett, "I should imagine the bulk under water would create certain disturbances of the ocean that might cause currents that would bring anything coming within their influence toward the vortex—by which I mean the island. That sounds as vague as my knowledge of physics but it's a sort of theory. It doesn't make much difference. It is simpler and perhaps wiser to attribute it all to Providence. Here we are."

"And here we are likely to remain. Don't you think we ought to build a beacon here and have fire-making materials ready in case we sighted sail or smoke? A vessel might come this way. We ought to have a lookout, too. And another one on that cape to the north."

"Did you say you were going to haul up the wood?" asked Malone of Bowman.

"I'll do my share. Suppose a ship should come along and we never know it, nor they dream we were stranded here? My ——!" Bowman stood with clenched fists and staring eyes; his jaws clenched so that the muscles of his face bulged out. The rest shared his emotions variously.

"Is there any way of calculating where we are, Brett?" demanded Tully. Brett shrugged his shoulders.

"I'll tell you what I have been able to figure out. Add to that the fact that we are on an island. We'll have to climb to the rim of the crater to be dead sure what lies south of us. I know something about sailing and I have dabbled with navigation. But we have no instruments. We can't fix our longitude, we have no means of knowing how far we are from the South American coast which is, I think, the nearest land, somewhere to the east. The noon shadow is very slight, which would place us down toward the Equator.

"At the North Pole the North Star is approximately overhead—ninety degrees above the horizon. Farther south you get, the lower in the heavens it shows. By guessing at its angle you might be able to guess about your latitude—somewhere near it. I don't know just where the curve of the earth—as you travel south—would shut off the view of the North Star and of the Dipper wheeling about it—but I haven't been able to locate either.

"Perhaps the North Star is below the horizon and that part of the constellation showing at this time of year is one I can't recognize. I don't, anyway. I don't know anything about the stars of the southern hemisphere. I don't know if I could pick out the Southern Cross—as we discussed the other night. We landed on the north of the island and so far I haven't noticed the southern sky at night. But I doubt if it would help any."

Walker was standing gazing seaward with his face twisted in the expression that was half question and half grin as if the matter of living was a humorous enigma. He whistled softly yet shrilly between his teeth.

It's a long way to Tipperary, it's a long way to go;
It's a long way to Tipperary, to the sweetest girl I know.

There are some songs to which the words are as familiar as the tune. Brett saw Tully's face working with emotion. Wallaby Brown had caught up a corner of his lower lip and his eyes were screwed close. Tully's eyes were frankly moist, and O'Neill's handsome face registered real tragedy.

Perhaps he had so much of the actor in him that he was forced to exaggerate dramatic moments in speech or action but, to Brett, who felt—with a passing wonderment, that he did not share their sensations—O'Neill's expressed sentiment was not all unreal. Malone, with the Irishman's susceptibility, responded to the marching lilt that came out of his own country, but his pose was defiant, his face cynical. Bowman had turned his back.

"For God's sake, Walker," cried O'Neill, "not that, man, not that!"

"Not what?" Walker's whistle had been subconsciously inspired.

"What you are whistling. Might as well be *Home Sweet Home*."

"Oh, might it? There weren't nothing sweet about my 'ome. But—" He gazed at the others and nodded comprehension. "I'm sorry."

"Home!" said Bowman. "How are we ever going to get there? To be penned up here for life, away from—everything. We can't wait for some ship to come along. It might never arrive. Life going on—over there—and we out of it." Here was the cry of youth for pleasure, for sex, for the sheer joy of living. It was tragic enough. "We've got to build a ship," he declared.

"A ship!" laughed Malone. "A fine ship you'll be building when you can't even cut down a tree. I should think you'd had enough of ships for a while. I'm as strong for gettin' back as you are, Bowman, but I like to know where I am going and who's running things right. Would you tackle it on a raft? How about your grub? What'll you do, fill up on water before you start? Ship! ——!"

"It can be done. Can't it?" He appealed to Brett. .

"It might. We've got to go a long way before we could build a ship. A plank is a problem without tools. We have no nails, no sail material, no facilities for carrying provisions. But it might be done. When Bligh, of the *Bounty*, was put into an open boat by the mutineers with eighteen of his crew who remained faithful, they had something less than a hundred and thirty pounds of bread, a few pieces of pork, a little rum and wine and less than thirty gallons of water. About five days, full rations. The boat was twenty-three feet long. They caught two small birds. They used rainwater. They were thirty days before landing on New Holland.

"They had to go on and, by this time, the only good watch they had stopped. They reached Timor, their destination, after a grueling run of three-thousand-six-hundred and eighteen miles in an open boat in forty-one days. Counting their landing at New Holland, they averaged a hundred miles a day. True, they had a quadrant and compass; they were expert mariners—most of them officers of the transport—but they were deep-laden and overcrowded. The boat was probably a good one.

"I don't think we can be anywhere near that distance from land. Bligh, in his narrative of the voyage from Tahiti to Timor, states that they passed constantly in sight of islands but dared not land upon them for fear of the natives. On the fifteenth day they went close to the New Hebrides. They were sailing west. We should go east. There are no islands likely to be east of us where, if there are inhabitants, they would not be friendly. What men have done others can do. The boat is our handicap. To make planks without a saw, to make a saw without metal, to fasten the planks together."

"If we are near the equator, according to the shadow, why don't we see more tropical growth?"

"We may find some yet, Tully, after we've explored a bit. I know it isn't very hot on the Galapagos Islands and they are right under the equator. I know that it is likely to be rainy weather on the equatorial belt most of the year. I know that the trees and plants on the Galapagos, which are tropical, are supposed to have been imported by man. The native growth is different from that of the nearest mainland, Ecuador, and they find giant tortoises there four to five feet long and weighing half a ton.

"There are no similar tortoises on the mainland nor any remains of them. The tortoises can float but they can't swim. Scientists claim they are evidence that the islands were once part of another continent. We may be on a similar formation. We are not on the Galapagos, for that is a group with the islands in plain sight of each other. I happen to know all this because a man who wrote a treasure story for a magazine I edited, placed his plot on the Galapagos, where he lived for a time. He came into the office and we had dinner together. He told me about his experiences and, at the time, I envied him."

"I'd like to find one of those 'arf a ton tortoises," said Walker. "The Lord Mayor 'ud 'ave nothing on us. The shell 'ud be prime for cooking. Some reptile, to furnish soup-meat and the pot to cook it in. Wot?"

"Say we happened to be six hundred miles east of the Galapagos," insisted Bowman. "Say we sailed east and missed them. If we sailed right into the dawn we couldn't miss South America, could we? Then we could coast north to some port."

"First build the boat," said Brett. "The sort we could put together with the best of tools would have to depend on wind and we might run into calms lasting a week. We'd have to tack and sometimes we'd lose a lot of leeway with a head wind. I'm not trying to discourage you but we've got to go slow, it seems to me."

"Go slow!" cried O'Neill. "By the time I get back I may be an old man! You fellows may think it's a snap to star in the films but I've worked like a dog to get where I am."

"Think of the advertising you'll get," jeered Malone. "You'll be able to bill yourself as the Wild Man from Borneo. Take care of your beauty, O'Neill. It's losin' out with the girls that's worryin' you, I'm thinkin'."

"What if it is? I'm not the only one. I want to live. You might as well be an oyster growing on a tree root as stuck on this dump. I want to live, I tell you—not exist," he exclaimed passionately.

"I've got a wife and kids. They'll be thinking I'm dead by now," said Wallaby Brown slowly. "I suppose we'll be reported lost at sea. One of the other boats may have got in. They'll not be so badly off. I've made good money and I 'aven't chucked it all away. I kept up good insurance. But they'll be missing me like I'm missing them.

"You chaps ain't married, I take it—except the professor. It's just girls to you chaps—girls and a' good time. It's wife to me—kiddies—a home. I'm going to make a stab at getting to 'em soon as I can, but I'm votin' with Mr. Brett. We got to go slow. We 'ad one taste of it in a small boat. Leave it to 'im and we'll 'ave a ship some'ow."

"Meantime," said Walker, "while there ain't no use in dodging the fact we're up against it, there's no sense to grouching. The beacon's a good idea. We'll build it. Let's go on to the top of this dump-'eap and see w'ot we can see. Then go down where we can get a drink of water and do some more exploring while it's light. The blooming island ain't more than five miles by three."

They started for the final sharp climb. Brett, watching them, realized that the professor was not the only man attacked by sickness. They were feverish with nostalgia—a disease that would be constantly recurrent and ever gaining in strength. For himself Brett felt no special twinge of home-sickness. The germ of adventure, so long dormant, was spreading through him. To fight against Nature in its own stronghold, to render it sub-servient, stimulated him. There were men born that way, he supposed, men with a touch of the Viking, the pioneer, the hermit even.

He missed his books, certain congenial cronies, his pipe, music, the-aters; but there were compensations. In him was welling up capacity to meet obstacles and conquer circumstance. He felt reserves of strength and confidence, an independence and a rising flood of health and optimism in his own resources, despite all their privations, that was new to him, that he accepted as an heir coming into his own kingdom. The little island, thrust up from the measureless sea, with all its pride of greenery, its grades of life, inspired him. It was a challenge! He was man, and therefore master of such things.

Some day this tiny dominion would be discovered, put to its ultimate uses, set down on the maps. Those who came would find that he had been there before them and, like a true frontiersman, had not neglected his op-portunities. It was the mission of civilized man to carry civilization. It was not a prison in his eyes, a place to mope in and bewail fate if escape was not opportune. With the others it might well be different.

If they looked to him to devise a means of escape he would set his wits to that end, but he was not at all sure of the feasibility of ship-build-ing. The risks of a voyage without compass or quadrant in such a green lumber craft as they could build would be enormous. but they did not af-fright him. He simply did not weigh them in the same proportions as the others who wanted to live. *This* was life!

It did not take long to go round the upper end of the crevasse and scramble up the lip of the actual crater, probably the final cauldron in which the eruption material that had gone to the island's making had boiled and overflowed. There was not much to look at. A pit with steeply sloping sides of cinders through which were thrust here and there pro-jections of lava rock, gray and red and black.

Brett had expected a deeply exposed core, a vertical shaft reaching into the bowels of the heap, but it was choked a hundred feet down by a rubble of scoriae where the chimney had fallen in upon itself after the fire had died.

He looked south. The land ran out to a sharp promontory, barren with slag, a subsidiary crater occupying most of it, a cone about a quarter of the size of the one on which they stood. Beyond—the sea. No land, nothing but blue, shimmering sea and blue sky with masses of pearly cumulus clouds.

North they obtained a better view of the upper end of their home canyon, seeing clear over the spires of the forest. They could trace the source of their river and they saw now that the stream that ran south through the seeming swamp lands was a tributary of it, flowing down from a saddle of land.

East—Tully suddenly stiffened and pointed.

"Look! On the other side of the round bay. *Smoke!*"

They gazed breathless at the little column of vapor, blue white against the shadowed side of the far crater. It rose steadily from a mass of vegetation, close down by the water and plumed out until it faded mistily. Conjecture ran wild, concentrated in two possibilities. Another of the boats from the wreck had landed on the opposite side and the crew established themselves as they had done, unconscious of other existence. Or it was the fire of natives—presumably savage in this far off spot.

The first—hope backing it—seemed the more probable, as they discussed it. Their river was the larger. Surely they would have found traces of visitation, if not of habitation, by natives. And savages would surely have known, of their landing and attempted—armed as they would be, curious as they would be—either to meet or attack them.

It was a surmise they did not dare to leave unproven. Friend or wild foe it was impossible to rest unsatisfied. They had weapons of a sort; they would go cautiously.

The thick forest covering the eastern side of the crater offered good cover. It reached down to the nearer margin of the bay where the smoke showed. Doubtless the more brilliant verdure, that looked comparatively flat from the height, would develop into trees and bush growth. Along the stream there were indications of loftier vegetation. Walker's estimate of distance seemed fair.

They had several hours of daylight and they had brought along some food. Water was the first consideration. They decided to travel down a fin-like ridge that would bring them to where the canyon curved and the river looped, with the cliffs receding and lessening. They could follow up the river to the tributary and continue along the eastern bank of the latter.

Two hours should make it, they agreed, though excitement discounted distance. They set out eagerly down the ridge into the shade of the forest. Among these conifers grew trees with more lacy foliage; the undergrowth was thicker and many creepers twined overhead so that the sun was shut out. There was a comforting lack of thorny growths and they made good progress, guessing the general direction by the trend of the shadows whenever a slight clearing gave them opportunity of observation. Birds of brilliant plumage flew overhead—ring-doves and small parrots in blue and crimson, cooing and chattering.

They came across a trail, hard trodden, narrow, leading downward toward the river which they could now glimpse occasionally. Along this they proceeded cautiously. It might have been made by man or by beasts, none of them was woodsman enough to determine that in the absence of clear signs until they came to a fern-circled pool, cool and clear. The soil was clayey and at one place imprinted with hoof-marks, evidently those of wild hogs.

There was a second, shallower spring where they had wallowed. The clear water indicated that it had not recently been disturbed but they stopped to listen before they drank, trying to see through the brush, seeing nothing, hearing nothing, to their relief. A wild boar, resenting intrusion, would not be a pleasant customer to meet; a herd would rout them, tusks against spears and clubs, possibly tree them for hours. Brett knew that there were kinds of swine indigenous to America, from Arkansas southward. These might be the same peccaries. Original inhabitants of this nubbin of a vanished continent.

Their thirst quenched, they pushed on refreshed, resolving to return to this trail and make pitfalls in it and about the spring as well as in the clearing where O'Neill had discovered the uprooted yams. Those yams Brett resolved to cultivate.

The forest thinned out; the conifers gave way to many varieties of trees. For the first time fan palms showed, dwarf palmettos rather, since they grew only as ground shrubbery. The fibrous leaves of this gave promise of the most likely material so far discovered for twine and rope making, for hats, baskets and fans. Tully discovered some pale golden globes gleaming among glossy leaves. Forcing his way through the tangle he came back triumphantly bearing two great shaddocks that weighed nearly ten pounds apiece, so far as they could guess.

"Some grapefruits!" he cried jubilantly. They opened up one of them and found the pulp crimson, slightly acid, delicious, though the partitions were bitter as quinine. Malone was less fortunate. Spying a bush laden with fruit in the shape of small oblong cylinders, growing in pairs, scarlet in color, he sampled, cautiously enough, and spat out furiously. It was a pepper allied to tabasco, if not actually that plant.

One other welcome find they made as they emerged from the trees into guava scrub, fighting their way through the jungle of it but picking the pink and white pulped fruit and eating it avidly. They reached the marshlands, thick set with tall reeds and great masses of lavender and white iris. The ground was moist, soggy but not so much as to appear dangerous. Their feet sank slightly into the spongy soil but it seemed as if the lake they had seen from the crater drained most of the superfluous water. There were occasional mounds, grass grown. From one of these they caught the gleam of the bay they were bound for and, on the far shore, the steady thread of smoke that plumed out and faded into mist.

They were well into the swamp before they noticed that their guess as to the thoroughness of the lake drainage was not a good one. Little runnels of water began to appear more and more frequently, showing abruptly among the reeds that were shoulder high. Most of these sloughs they leaped, others they were forced to wade and found the bottom treacherous. The mire was soft and they began to slosh through it ankle deep, then halfway to the calf, with more and more difficulty of extrication. Feet came clear with a sucking noise and the feeling of a broken grip that plucked steadily at every stride.

Mosquitoes—they had not noticed any on the crater or in the woods, even at the spring—hummed and burred about them more and more thickly as if they were assembling from all over the morass. They fanned at them with the palmettos they had torn up but the insects were persistent and soon so thick that they appeared like black clouds, stinging every portion of exposed skin, lancing through the thin clothing. The bites swelled rapidly, showing white blisters on the sun-scorched skin. The places itched intolerably before they began to burn. The increasing irritation sank deeper than the skin, their blood seemed to boil, their bodies to be afire with fever.

The worst danger that threatened was blindness. A few more stings on the eyelids would leave them plunging, staggering through the mire, lost to all direction, floundering, falling into sloughs or pools, exhausted at last, not to arise. It was a very real peril.

Wallaby Brown, blundering on with his face protected by hands and crossed forearms, broke through first to the lake, stumbling, pitching forward on all fours into the water while, with a whirring roar of swiftly driven pinions, up rose a flock of ducks, squawking in protest, mounting, wheeling, forming into "V" companies under their leaders and rocketing away. They were too persecuted for the time to see the irony of this sudden disclosure of a food supply that was beyond any efforts of theirs to secure. All waded deep into the lake and ducked under its surface to get rid of their persistent enemies, waiting for them to come up again.

Brett caught inspiration from a glimpse of Brown, pawing at his tortured face with his hands that were thickly coated with the slime of the lake's bottom.

"Mud's better than clothes," he said. "It'll dry on us like armor." They were swift to grasp the hope and waded out again, stripping themselves and daubing their bodies thick with the sticky stuff, plastering on the ooze, regardless of its odors, smearing it from where the hair ended over face and neck and ears down to the soles of their feet. Parts of their clothing they made turbans of, rolling up their pajamas until they were merely loin-cloths.

The mud relieved the pain almost instantly. It baffled the mosquitoes. It restored their equanimity so that they were able to roar at the ludicrous appearance they cut, dripping ooze and slime as they started for a second coating of security. It dried swiftly in the sun rays, now beginning to slant from the westward, dried like an unwholesome rind.

"Some war-paint," cried Walker. "Like Hepps' Cocoa, grateful and comforting. Hey! Come 'ere—careful as you go. Look at that!"

The original Crusoe, staring at the footprint in the sand, was not thrown into greater consternation than they as they crowded together, held back by Walker's extended arm from destroying the trace he had found. There in the mud was a big splay-footed track, heel and toes and even the bridging flat instep where the moist dirt had received it. Ahead of that perfect slot was the mark of a knee, the depression of the deeper imbedded toes and sale of the mating foot. Here a barbarian had evidently gone down on one knee and scooped up the lake water for a drink. So the runes read to the group of white men, checked in their mirth, reduced to whispers, looking fearfully about them.

Judging by the size of the track, the savage was a man as large as any of them. Even now he might be ambushed in the reeds, drawing a poisoned arrow to its head or setting a tiny venomed dart within a blowpipe.

Imagination never runs riot more wildly, more alarmingly, than in the bush or jungles of a savage land whose inhabitants are unknown. The air was charged with menace, the wind whispering through the water-grasses seemed the rustle of a gathering foe. Fear gripped all of them, their rude weapons seemed useless as toys. Their brains, with the reins of emotions cast loose by the shocked wills, stampeded to thoughts of torture, stake and fire, the death-ovens of cannibals! Then they rallied.

"They are not about," said Brett, his voice pitched low, filled with relief. "The ducks flew from us. They would not have been settled down if anyone was near."

"Unless they were lying mighty low, waiting for a shot at them," said Tully, shattering security.

"It isn't one of our own tracks?" asked O'Neill.

"No one's been here but me," declared Walker. "It ain't mine. I've got on my sneakers and that 'oof's twice my size. Here's my trail. And I was all alone. We'd better get out of here."

"You're right," said Brett crisply. The combination of the savage spoor and the smoke column filled him with a premonition of dread. He wanted to get back to the cave. Time had flown while they splashed through the swamp, the sun was getting perilously low and they could not tell how soon they might be able to work their way back to the highlands. Apprehension for the professor assailed him. Reluctant as he was to return without solving the question of the smoke, it seemed, in the face of things, a dangerous thing to attempt that night, dangerous to stay away from their own base after dark. There was the hunting pack, the boars and now—tribesmen. A thought struck him.

"It couldn't be Wolf?"

"He was going to take the raft and fish down-stream," said Malone. "What would he be wandering off here by himself for when he told me he didn't want to go away from camp? He was crazy to fish."

Brett turned away, the flimsy hope dissolved. Remembering the lay of the land as they had surveyed it from the crater he struck out toward the saddle of land that had appeared as the source and watershed of the two streams. From there they could follow the ravine to camp or keep along the high cliffs if the going was better. No one mentioned the professor, but it was evident that they were all keen to return. Their plastered faces showed no expression; but their eyes, curiously, comically plain, stared out of the masks anxiously.

The dried mud served them well though the mosquitoes sought every crack in the armor. Occasionally they renewed the coating as they went along, floundering through the swamp that seemed to have reserved its worst perils for their homeward trip. Walker sank to his waist in a quickmire and Brett went as deep trying to haul him out. They formed a chain and achieved a rescue after great effort, forced to make a long detour about the treacherous strip. Its farther margin proved quaking and spongy. Every step was to the knees for a while, draining them of their strength.

They won free at last, gaining a slope where guavas grew. These they gathered and ate while they rested a short time, limited by the threat of the shadows. The umbra of the crater was flung over the eastern half of the island; the sun was hidden behind its rim. Night was coming swiftly, the final rush imminent. It grew perceptibly cooler on the edge of the morass. Filled with the pulp, refreshed a little, they picked up their weapons and hurried on through the fringe of the forest. Where the sky showed, it flamed with sunset and afterglow that quickly faded. They came out of the woods above the canyon and, in the last twilight, made their way toward its cliffs.

Every moment they had dreaded to hear a yell, the patter of rushing feet, the whirr of arrows—or—worse—to see some of them fall stricken by an unsensed foe, smitten from ambush, pricked by a deadly dart puffed from bush or bough. The atmosphere was charged with a presentiment of evil, for themselves on the home trail, and for Harland and Wolf, surprised at the cave and along the river.

They crossed a bare stretch to the margin of the ravine at a half run.

Here, if ever, as they broke cover, they would be attacked. The sweat of reaction broke out on them as they found themselves unmolested. They must have passed unseen, the prints must have been those of a lone warrior. Yet he might have warned the tribe who would, savage fashion—as they imagined it—hold a pow-wow and a war-dance before they gave battle to the white invaders.

The moon rolled up from behind the eastern cone as they halted for a moment to get their wind and decided upon the best course. The cliffs were from fifty to a hundred feet high and precipitous, offering no immediate and easy chance of descent to the bed of the canyon where the river ran in a rocky trough. Trees grew in clumps on the margin, with strips of tall grass and coverts of shrubbery. Hundreds of uprooted trees were stranded here and there. The evening wind drew up the ravine like a draft up a chimney. It brought the sound of the waterfall, beyond that, faintly, the drumming of the surf. And——

They became rigid, standing like stone figures, listening.

From across the canyon where the cliffs were broken down into slopes and terraces and the forest mounted steadily to the seaward precipices, there came the swelling uproar of the pack—louder and closer—a brutish blend of howl and bay—eager, defiant of concealment, knowing the cry of the hunt carried terror to all living things, striking in to jellying marrow, robbing fleet limbs of speed, paralyzing instinct and destroying cunning.

It expanded to a vicious, blood-curdling howl, then died to a silence yet more terrible. The mind's eye beheld the ravening brutes coming on, fleet to follow the scent they had struck, with jaws slavering in anticipation as the nostrils widened to the pungent particles that betrayed their victims. Heads pressed close to the dirt the better to enjoy the odor, or flung up in bestial delight of the chase that would end in the slashing, clawing, rending kill, the lapping of hot blood, the gulping of quivering flesh. They shrank down close to the ground, grasping their weapons. Atop the steep cliffs they were immune. Intent upon the warm trail they were following it was improbable that the pack would sight them; the wind precluded discovery from smell.

The moon soared up, full and brilliant, unclouded, strong enough to hold much of the color of the ground and trees.

There was one solo howl—questing, anxious. Another. Then full cry again as the fault was bridged. The next instant the pack broke into view, going so swiftly across a slope that they were merely a close running blur of great brutes disappearing into a draw. They were silent now, save for an occasional quivering whimper of impatience. The five men squatted tense, waiting for them to cross a stretch of rock at the foot of the draw.

They came racing out into the moonlight straight on to the river and broke up into groups, individuals, roaming swiftly here and there, turning sharply, nosing the ground. One or two lapped at the water. One great beast sat back on its haunches, lifted its nose and howled. With the pose the sound became instantly translatable, the identity of the creatures revealed. They were hounds, enormous dogs, larger than Great Danes, short-furred, lop-eared, long of limb and of their whip-stock tails. Baffled wails broke out as they followed the example of their leader, making the night hideous with their clamor. In the clear light Brett caught the gleam of teeth. He fancied he could see the lolling tongues in the dripping jaws.

The leader crouched and sprang, magnificent, clean-leaping as a cougar, bounding across to a rock that stemmed the current, a clear jump of close to a score of feet. For a moment he stood with head up and one paw raised, frozen, sniffing with wrinkled muzzle.

Nothing came to him on the wind. He was soon satisfied that the quarry had not doubled—gone down stream. Without hesitation he jumped into the pool that was too wide for further leaping, swimming across swiftly, chest well out, shaking himself as he came out with a brilliant dazzle of the drops that flew from his body in the moonlight. He began to run about, casting for renewed scent.

It was intelligent but not marvelously so. Pigs would be expected to cross directly to the far side of a stream; they would not swim it. The wonder was that pigs crossed water that was so deep and swift. Animals in a wild state do many things the tamed varieties have forgotten about. A further surprise was the fact that the rest of the pack stayed across the river. Some of them even lay down, content to know that their leader was at work.

They were formidable looking brutes. Brett surmised that their presence proved the previous dwelling, or landing, of white men. But one could not be sure. No one was quite sure from whence the dog had originally sprung. Wild wolf, coyote, dingo, dholo, jackal, fox? Long-haired all these, with plumed tails. The island pack was short of hair, suiting the climate.

The first dog likely crossed the line between freedom and domestication with the first of the camp-fires, creeping in, urged by a strange tug to become friend and ally of this two-legged, upright walking god who could make flame. If wild dogs were tamed, so these, even if they were actually a primitive species, might be brought into camp, made comrades instead of enemies. It would seem good to have a dog or two about, Brett thought, and then necessity smiled grimly and whispered that they needed the hides for sandals, for clothing, for lashings and all uses of leather. Also they were a long, long way from being tamed; they would not be easy to conquer, even in a battle to the death.

The leader had found the scent again and he gave instant tongue that was taken up by the orchestra of the pack, leaping exultantly before they plunged into the water, one or two, more clumsily emulating the leap of their chief to the rock. Twenty-three of them, Brett counted, as they clove the stream with their powerful muscles, each swimming in independent course, emerging, shaking, finding the ground scent, forming into pack and then off up the ravine, closely running, side by side, silent again for the while, tails waving stiffly; the leader in front, nose to earth, muzzle swaying a little as he raced. They were lost in shadow, seen for a moment again in light and then they rounded a bend in the canyon. Their diabolical cry sounded as if the trail had yielded up a special burst of effluvium. Then they were gone, utterly.

"I'd sure hate to have *that* bunch after me, with no trees in sight," said Bowman.

"It would be a battle royal between them and wild boars—if the number was equal." This from Tully.

"Dogs take care of that. They hunt in a pack by instinct. And they do all the hunting. And we thought they were lions and were going to rig up a deadfall! You'll not catch those chaps that way. They wouldn't climb out along a log to reach the bait," said Bowman.

"We'll 'ave to look out for our larder. We'll 'ave trouble with those beggars," said Walker. " 'Spose they are dorgs but they're bigger'n any ruddy 'ound I ever saw. Bigger'n Shetland ponies. Travel fast, don't they?"

A sound like a medley of hunting horns, blown very far away, came faintly to them against the wind. Its note changed.

"Made their kill," said Brett. "Wonder what keeps their numbers down and why they haven't killed off all the pigs?"

"Dog eat dog," suggested Malone.

They had come to a cutaway in the cliff, leading down to the ravine. This they negotiated and passed swiftly along to the waterfall, though the way was made devious by rock masses and the jumble of stranded timber.

Brett gazed anxiously up-slope toward the cave. That side of the canyon was in darkness, unillumined by the moon. The fire should have showed ruddily and cheerfully as a lighted window. But there was no sign of it at all.

The apprehension he had felt swelled into certainty. Disaster of some sort had happened the moment they had left in force. The professor—Wolf—were they murdered or had they been carried off for savage deviltry? Brett gulped hard.

His own blood tingled at the way his comrades went up the slope without hesitation. So some of them had topped the trenches. It warmed him to feel that he was unafraid though he did not stay for analysis of his emotion. Vengeance was the main factor of that. Professor Harland, old enough to be the father of many of them, weak and sick but game through and through, lying there mutilated, or—?

The cavern gaped like a silent, tongueless mouth. Its roof reflected a feeble glow from an almost dead fire. There was a lot of wood on the floor and Brett, first across the threshold, tossed some of the smaller boughs on the fire with some bits of bark that flared up; revealing the prostrate figure of Professor Harland, lying, not on the ferns, but on the bare dirt, his scanty gray hair catching the light, his arms outflung, his body ominously still.

Brett kneeled beside him, running his hands over him. There was no blood, the limp body seemed whole enough. He caught a faint pulsing at the wrist, a suggestion of a heartbeat. Some one had got the fire roaring. Malone was beside Brett with an improvised torch.

"Sure he ain't hurt," he said. "They must have clubbed him. Say, look at his throat." On the withered neck, bronzed with exposure, the marks of clutching fingers were plain in purple bruises.

"I'd like to get at the one who did that," growled Malone. "I'd twist his neck off." There was a note in his voice that made Brett glance at him curiously, a note of regret born of real affection hallowing his rage. "What I can't make out," he went on, "is why they didn't——" He broke off short. Brett had taken a wetted bit of bark cloth from Tully, and Bowman had brought more water in his palms. They chafed his wrists, bathed face and neck, tried to get some water between the jaws, clenched as tightly as a sprung trap.

"Wasn't natives did this." announced Malone suddenly. "Some one's turned his pockets inside out. Your money's gone, Brett. It was Wolf turned this trick, blast him! I ought to have seen he wasn't comin' out of his trance like he used to. He's gone plumb, stark crazy. And he's scragged the prof for the dough."

"What good would it do 'im?" asked Brown.

"Not a bit. I tell you he was crazy. Me too, I'm as big a fool as he is. He wanted me to run off with him and do in all of you. He got the idea in his head that this was *his* island. Bolshevik stuff. Brett here was tryin' to be a Czar. We was to kill all of you, get the money. That's how I knew he'd gone off his nut, acting as if the money was any good. But I thought he'd come round and I let him rave.

"Now he's done in the prof and I'll get him or chase him into the sea for the sharks. We *got* to get him or he'll sure raise — with us. Lucky he can't buy bombs with that money. He's a crazy Bolshevik—worse than any of 'em, because he's madder. And he had to pick the prof becos he had the money. I'll mend his brains before morning. I'll scramble 'em."

He broke off into a long string of virulent invective, rudimentary, forecastle and fire-room blasphemy qualified by the evident grief back of it that was the bellows blowing up his determination for revenge.

"You can't get him tonight, Malone," said Brett. "Besides, the dogs may have been after him. They may have got him. They might you. That was his footprint by the lake, his fire smoke across the bay. There are no savages here after all. Wolf took fire with him from this one. He could have carried tinder and kept it going easily enough. He was cunning enough for that."

"He must have tackled the professor soon after we left to get that far. Premeditated the whole thing," said Tully. "I hope the dogs get him."

"He wasn't afraid of the dogs," said Malone. "Not even when he thought they were lions. He thought he was king of the whole ruddy castle. And he made a sucker out of me. I—"

A sigh came from the professor and they increased their efforts, rubbing ankles as well as wrists, applying friction to his soles and palms. Brett raised his head and shoulders on his knees. The sick man swallowed a little water, choked, swallowed some more and opened his eyes. He tried to speak but only made strange clucking noises.

"You take it easy," said Brett. "You'll soon be all right now. It was Wolf who did it?" The professor nodded weakly and closed his eyes again. They put him on fern litter closer to the fire. He began to breathe naturally; pulse and heart resumed almost normal action. Ease of mind from knowing himself surrounded by friends contributed toward the sleep that claimed him as the rest sat round the fire and ate, discussing Wolf.

That he must not be allowed at large they soon determined. If he was mad and therefore not responsible, nevertheless he must be prevented from committing irresponsible acts though he might not be really guilty of crime or deserving of punishment. The arguments flamed hot concerning penalty.

"What are you goin' to do with him, then?" demanded Malone. "Keep him tied up? Feed him like a kid in a high chair? I've seen his kind go bad before, from stoke-room heat. Brain goes rotten like spoiled fruit. Maggots in it. Thinks he owns the island and he'll take every chance he gets to kill us off. One at a time if he can't do any better. Either you bump him off or keep him caged up. If you don't, you might as well commit suicide. He'll get us sooner or later. It's up to me. I ought to have tumbled to him. He did his best to murder the prof. My fault. All right. I'll even it up—and I'll bring back the money. Not that it's much good now but it might be some day, at that."

"We've got to give him the chance of getting his wits back," said Brett. "Even if we have to confine him."

"You never brought a nut back to his senses by tying him up," demurred Malone. "I suppose you'll vote me down, as usual, but you'll be sorry for it. He chokes the prof and you're going to slap him on the wrist and say 'naughty.' Give him a soft snap of no work and plenty of grub and, if he ever breaks loose, he'll bash in the back of your head with a rock."

"I didn't know the professor was such a special friend of yours, Malone," said O'Neill. "I wonder whether you'd have been as anxious to get Wolf if it had been one of the rest of us?"

"You've said it yourself. No. Why the prof? Because he's the salt of the earth. Chuck-full of education and don't think himself a bit better than the other guy. Talks to me man to man, all the same I was his own brother. The rest of you are almighty condescending but you think yourselves a cut above Malone the Boiler-Feeder.

"The prof is gamer than the whole bunch of you and he's the same every second of the twenty-four hours. He's like first-class linoleum, is the prof. The pattern lasts all the way through till the stuff's worn out. If he croaks I'll see the Slovak pays for it, vote or no vote. You can hold your ballot and to — with you!"

He left the group and went to the front of the cave. It was a curious twist for Malone, the affection he held for the professor against his ultra socialistic principles as applied toward the rest of them. That he blamed himself entirely for the happening was plain. He had known Wolf far better than any of them. But he had not been able to judge the sudden atavism, the result of the successive shocks that had upset Wolf's mental balance, never very sure, and thrust him into brutedom.

Wolf could fend for himself now that he had fire. Whether he could protect himself against the hunting pack, the boars, the hazards of the island life, was a question. How far he might injure them was another. The debate ended with a resolve to attempt to secure him, to render him the best possible treatment, starting for that purpose the next day, leaving half their number at the cave. The place where they had seen the smoke was to be their objective. This was not unanimous. Walker, O'Neill and Brown were for leaving him to his own fate, provided the professor was not seriously injured. If Harland should happen to die, they believed that Wolf should be put out of the way.

" 'E's a murderer, any way you look at it," pronounced Walker. "And a mad murderer is much worse than a sane one, to my mind. We've got to look out for ourselves. An eye for an eye, a life for a life, I say. But I said I'd go with the majority and I do. I'm telling you one thing, and that is I'm jolly well glad that was Wolf's 'oof-mark and 'is smoke. I've been seeing cannibals all night. We've got troubles enough outside of that."

They all subscribed to that, with certain reservations. It was not positive that Wolf had made footprint or fire. Tomorrow's exploration should clear up that. While they were hunting Wolf they would cover the island and determine whether there were others who claimed ownership. Doubt on that point meant persistent unrest by day and night.

CHAPTER IX.
MAN HUNTING.

MALONE WAS GONE the next morning before any of the others awakened. He had taken with him some cold food and the special weapon he had made from a jagged fragment of flint, bound into a cleft stick with vines. Wolf had made himself a similar one.

For a few moments they debated a question propounded by O'Neill. Was Malone genuine in his denunciation of Wolf? Had he not gone off to join him after all? They decided in the negative.

"Malone hates better than he likes," said Brett. "He would not have faked his feeling for Professor Harland."

"I don't know about that," countered O'Neill. "He admitted he was practically plotting with Wolf. Wolf may have gone off half-cocked and Malone taken the position he did so as to get a chance to sneak off and join him."

"In which case we are liable to find it out before the day's over," said Tully. "Who's going to form the home guard?"

They split their forces, three and three. Brett, Wallaby Brown and Tully to the trail. Walker, Bowman and O'Neill to stay behind, to watch over the professor and to provide food and wood.

Brett determined to avoid the swamp as much as possible. The big crater and the one back of it, except for the portion of the first covered with forest, did not need re-exploration on account of their barren, waterless slopes. He led the way over the back trail of the night before up to the place where they had watched the pack cross the river and then continued up the canyon along the top of the ever lessening cliffs. The canyon became a wide and shallow valley covered with long, slippery grasses, treeless. Through this they trudged in single file. There were no mosquitoes, which was a small blessing.

They reached a saddle of land, more or less rocky, with clumps of trees like cedars, distorted by the wind, the home stream flowing in a narrow channel through the plateau with occasional willows on the banks. More willows marching off at right angles and to the south seemed to mark the course of the stream they sought. This proved to be true and they traveled at good speed through fairly open country, gradually descending, the circular harbor in plain view and the column of smoke still ascending. Malone presumably was ahead of them though he might have chosen a different route. He would likely make for the smoke, whether going to join Wolf or to attack him.

In turn this smaller stream entered a valley but the character of the country was different from the northern side of the island. Brett fancied it was in the lee of the prevailing winds. It was less rocky; no cliffs appeared. The swamp lay to their right, but the water, if it drained the morass, ran through solid soil. There were guavas for a while, then brush palms that merged into groves of shaddocks, giving place to broad-leafed shade trees with smooth-barked trunks, interlaced with creepers bearing flowers whose strong perfumes hung heavy on the air. It looked as if they might do better to select this side of their dominion for a home.

The chance that one of the boats might have landed and the survivors caused the smoke still lingered in their minds and they talked of it when they halted for a brief rest. But it was a slim one and none of them placed much confidence in it. When they marched it was in silence, each man deep in thought.

The valley commenced to descend toward sea level in a series of terraces, the stream cascading down. The coniferous forest on the eastern slope of the main crater began to invade this territory, closing in to the bay that now opened full to their view, the little river entering it fairly in the center of its curve. The undergrowth was generous, extending out from the trees, close to the margin of the stream. Much of it was high enough to conceal their progress.

They came to a knoll topped by a few tall evergreens and climbed it for a final observation. The sun poured down from a cloudless sky, there were only sounds of birds and the murmur of the cascades, the place seemed a virgin solitude. From the height they could see the entire beach of the natural harbor.

There was no sign of any boat or canoe, no sign of habitation but the smoke going up from the verdure at the foot of the crater that made up the entire eastern promontory, as they had viewed it from the island's highest point. There was no sign of Wolf, or of Malone. Small, stilt-legged birds like plover were stalking along the beach margin, sometimes wheeling in small flocks with plaintive cries but landing again.

"You'd think Wolf would mask his smoke," said Tully. "He must know we'd be after him."

Brett was thinking that and he nodded.

"He should, if cunning and madness go together," he assented. "Somehow that smoke doesn't look quite natural to me. Or too natural. The amount never varies. A man would have to be feeding it all the time. The closer we get the more it looks like steam to me. See the way it plumes out."

"A hot spring at the foot of the crater?"

"I'd place a bet on it if we had anything to wager. We'll soon see."

Within half an hour they reached the source of the smoke. The vegetation, made up largely of enormous ferns, ceased abruptly and they broke through to an oval depression at the foot of a wall of the taffy-like lava that had once poured over a cliff from a plainly marked flow extending to the rim of the crater. In the center of the hollow were rocks, piled up like a cairn, partly covered with lichens. From the middle of the pile vapor streamed up as if through a chimney. The air was moist and warm, there was a distinct smell and flavor of sulfur. Small rocks and pebbles covered with a yellow-white deposit marked where some overflow drained into the porous ground. On one side of the rocks they found a slightly steaming pool, scummy, malodorous.

"Rotten eggs," said Wallaby Brown, "is lavender beside it."

"It might help to cure Harland. It's a laxative. It would make him sweat out his fever. The Indians in California built wicker sweat-houses over springs like that. Now they house them at health resorts."

"Cure him?" Brown looked at Brett with a wry face. "I wouldn't touch that stuff if it cured hams!"

The three of them laughed in a mingling of relief and disappointment. If Wolf was not here, nor any survivors from the wreck, neither were there any savages.

"Vote we move over here," said Tully. "Better view, better harbor. Sandy beach. No mangroves, no mosquitoes, no—"

"No oysters."

"There might be turtles. Fishing ought to be good. Better entrance through that reef when we build our ship. That steam coming up through the rocks isn't sulfurous. I tried some of it where it had filled up a hollow. Spray from the jet, I mean. It tasted kind of flat, like warm water out of a rusty dipper. You know, I bet it's good medicine. We could boil our grub, take warm baths."

Tully was rapidly becoming enthusiastic. Brett saw still other advantages. For the moment Wolf faded into the background. The soil on this side of the island was indisputably richer, with plenty of level surfaces. It could be irrigated. Brett was not a practical agriculturist but every Californian knows something of the theory of irrigation.

A vision of crops and plantations persisted with him, obscuring the thought of escape that seemed paramount with the rest of them. To transplant the best of the fruits, the edible shrubs and roots, and improve them—the ducks in the lake swamp had been feeding on wild rice, as Brett knew from his cruising and shooting days about the Sacramento sloughs. It all rose in his mind's eye, enticing. It was as attractive to him as the chance of a big job of puddle engineering is to a small boy, plus the man's enlarged capacities and recognition of utilities.

Brett had been pretty well shut in most of his life, he was beginning to realize. Civilized man might ultimately come to a diet of nitrogenous tablets, concentrated fats and sugars produced in factories under the superintendence of expert chemists, while the tilling of fields, the planting of orchards and vineyards, the tending of sheep and cattle vanished. But that was a long way off.

Man still was close to the soil. The majority of men were agriculturists, not one man in every thousand who did not long to dig earth, smell it, see things grow, if only in a back-lot garden. Part of the curse of Adam, Brett reflected smilingly, a curse that was also a beneficence. This was his first opportunity.

"The stream's smaller. There's 'ardly any driftwood round 'ere. If we cut wood you've got to float it across the bay. And 'ow about our fish-weir we've been breaking our backs over?"

Brown's objections broke in on Brett's musing.

"We can settle the moving question later," he suggested. "There's no sign of Wolf in this direction. Maybe Malone's had better luck. We might go round by the beach to see if there are any tracks and strike back home through the forest. I'm not keen to tackle the swamp. I don't imagine Wolf will elect to make that his headquarters. If he does I'd be inclined to leave him to the mercy of the mosquitoes."

The beach was pleasant walking. For much of their day's marching they had been able to dispense with the makeshift clumsy sandals. They fancied their feet were gradually hardening. Certainly the mud plasters of the day before, remnants of which still clung to them, had had a healing influence. The sea was shallow, sparkling and tempting, and they took an invigorating bath in the shore surf. The ocean bottom was the finest of coral grit with myriads of shells ground into infinitesimal fragments of iridescence.

While they were still in the water Tully excitedly pointed out a moving object on the beach, a rounded, perambulating shell that was unmistakably a turtle. They splashed out at top speed but the reptile was too swift for them, scuttling fast on its flippers and gaining the water before they could cut it off.

"Been laying eggs," Brown suggested. They followed the trail of the flippers and lost it in long trails of beach-vines.

"In the stories," said Brett, "in *all* the stories, the shipwrecked hero turns up the round, leathery-skinned eggs with unfailing precision and saves the life of the heroine and all the ship's company. It is easy to do it in print and on the film. As first-class castaways we are a failure. And if that turtle laid eggs round here she is a first-class sexton."

"Maybe it wasn't that kind of a turtle," Tully put in. "Anyway, there are turtles here and they do land on this beach. That's worth knowing.

"Seems to me I've read they only come out egg-laying at midnight, by moonlight. But we can make a watch-party and wait till one waddles out. Then we sprint out, lightly take the beast by the hind-nigh and the off-fore flipper *a la* Zybysco, give a dexterous twist—and there is Ma Turtle with her shoulders to the mat—as it were. Previously we have spotted where she deposited her eggs. Results—omelet for breakfast, soup for lunch, steak for dinner, calipash and calipee. A fine turtle-shell for a soup tureen, a washbowl, or beautiful tortoise-shell combs. Tortoise-shell toothpicks out of the trimmings. *Voila!*"

The nonsense carried off their chagrin. They ate cold fish and yams instead of the elusive eggs and finished circling the bay to a point opposite the smoke that had caused them such anxieties. Here the forest touched the lagoon. The thickets were so dense that they had to scout about to find an entrance that would not have to be won by an ax. Brett discovered the beaten trail, narrow, flattened by generations of hoofs and foot-pads of dogs and pigs.

It was doubtless made by the latter to reach the beach where they would find food along the margins, dead fish, occasional crabs, starfish— anything to relieve the monotony of yams. They might even enjoy a sea wallow. The dogs might like a sea swim, though Brett imagined they used the trail for grimmer purposes.

It was invitingly cool within.

At first the trees grew somewhat sparsely and the noon sun broke through in brilliant, dazzling pools of glare. But there was plenty of shade for the most part. For a while the trail skirted the forest, following the general contour of the land. Doves cooed and parrots chattered. They walked cautiously but at a good clip, ears alert, eyes glancing everywhere, their weapons tightly clutched.

Suddenly a flock of parrots came screaming down the green aisle, flying low, swerving off and up at sight of the three men, squawking angrily. Brett was in the lead. Brown and Tully ranged as close to him as the width of the path would allow and they advanced with slow wariness to discover what had disturbed the parrots.

The trail turned at a sharp tangent, rounding the buttresses of a great tree, its lower boughs curtained with creepers. They peered through this green screen and saw a man come limping down the path, clutching at the tree trunks for support, his head sunk low between his shoulders, groaning in evident pain. He stopped, leaning against a pole. He looked anxiously behind him, then sighted in front, shading his eyes against a sun spot.

It was Malone, weaponless, discomfited, injured. Brett called to him, then stepped out in plain sight, followed by the other two. Malone croaked a greeting—then—as they came up—

"Where can I get water, for the love of God!"

Tully gave him a couple of guavas he had been saving and Malone bit deep into the pulp. He was in sorry shape. His singlet was ripped clear of all selvage and one leg of his worn, stained dungarees was torn away close to his crotch. There was blood on one shoulder and his hair was matted with it. His left arm hung limp.

"Found Wolf?" asked Brown.

Malone spat out the rind of his guavas. "Found him? Blast him, he found me! I was coming through the woods, making for the bay and I was keeping my eyes peeled and not makin' any noise. The trees thin out a way back and I'd seen the blue water. All of a sudden I runs across a spring, like the one we saw yesterday. All marked up with pig-hoofs and dog feet. That wasn't all. It warn't quite clear, as if something had been drinking not long before. That made me extra careful and I'll tell you eyes and ears fair sprouted all over me when I see two footprints—same as we see at the lake. Identical. Then more of 'em—two or three. All comin' *to* the spring—none goin'. That puzzled me for a jiffy. Like a — fool I never thought to look *up*. Then there was a — of a racket of birds and I see, right there in the pool, Wolf, up in the boughs like a big gorilla. See his teeth and the whites of his eyes plain as if they was white pebbles at the bottom. He was grinning at me.

"He may have been friendly, savvy? He may have figured I'd come out to join him, like he's proposed, seein' I was alone. If I'd thought, I'd have jollied him along till I got a even chance with him. But I showed I was sore, and I was surprised an' so I sings out to him, 'Come down out of that, you ruddy murderer!' He comes, all right. His grin changed quick and he flings that club of his. It catches me on the top of my head and prit' nigh puts me out. The Wolf drops out of the tree and we're at it. He's got all the best of me from the start. I go down with his weight atop of me and I twist my arm under me. I get in one wallop, with my club, and he roars like a bull. Say, he's stronger than six ordinary men.

"He come down astride my shoulders and then he grabs my good arm with his two hands and scraps for my club. I won't let go and he can't make me, but he can break the handle—and he does. The rest is a whirl—all over the ground an' into the pool—with me fighting for life. That clip on the head had put me on the bum and I sure warn't gettin' any stronger.

Wolf gets hold of my ankles and gives me the leg-split. I thought he'd tear 'em apart. And *hurt?*

"I'm no squealer but there ain't a man alive that can stand that. It finished me. I flop, with him chokin' the breath out of me. Like a wild beast he was, snappin' his teeth. I thought he'd tear the flesh off me. Why he didn't finish me, I dunno. Maybe he thought he had. But, when I see light again, he's gone, up in his trees most likely. I get up but I can hardly walk. I'm through fighting for the day, or man huntin'. So I start down for the sea, half dizzy. I wasn't out long. The pool's still all muddy an' bloody when I leave it. Mebbe it's clear now an' I sure need a drink. Holy Saint Patrick, what I'd give for a *real* drink!"

The man-handling he had gone through had almost destroyed his locomotion, but his obstinate pride insisted that he could walk without help. He did accept a spear from Brown who had both that and his club, and he used this as a staff, walking between Tully and Brown.

They came to the spring, now fairly clear, and saw the trampled margin. To the best of their recollection the footprints that did not match Malone's, and were therefore Wolf's, duplicated those seen at the lake, which were pretty well printed in their minds. It seemed finally to dispose of the question of savages. There had evidently been a furious fight. Handicapped as he was, Malone had put up a good argument.

They all drank and they got Malone in as good shape as possible. The blow on the back of his head had been only a glancing one, causing a scalp wound and a terrific headache. The oiler complained but little. Trudging along as they struck deeper into the woods, traveling north and east toward the home canyon, their search extended to the boughs.

It appeared now that Wolf had not brought fire along with him but it was probable that while his wits had been, in one sense, dulled, in other ways they might be keen enough and he had seen the process of flint and stone. His tree progression might be a precaution against the dogs that might have been on his trail the night before, or a complete lapse, a reversion toward original type.

Malone stopped occasionally, trying to smother a groan. Wallaby looked him over. "Look 'ere, Malone," he said. "You'd better let us make a litter and carry you. You've been strained bad with that split-hold. You might 'ave got a rupture. What you want to do is to take it easy."

"I suppose you think you could have licked him one-handed, eh?" sneered Malone. His face was gray and haggard under its bristles, his eyes sunken in dark pits.

"Not a bit of it, pal. I bet you put up one — of a good scrap! But 'e got you foul. You take my advice——"

"I don't want it, nor your help either. From none of you," yapped Malone, forcing himself to stride on, stiff-legged, his good arm clinging to the spear. Brown shrugged his shoulders. He winked at Brett, which the latter interpreted as a prophecy that Malone would not last much longer on his own feet.

They entered a glade where a rocky outcrop made the soil too shallow for tree growth. The trees that circled it had dark, glossy leaves and were heavy with nuts, many of which were on the ground from ripeness or windfall. They seemed not unlike chestnuts; encased in a thick rind more like that of the walnut, the meat was sweet though hard and very oily. But the enormous number of crushed outer shells showed that the wild pigs made this a favorite feeding ground, munching the mast, ejecting the bitter rinds.

Crossing this Malone suddenly collapsed. Tully stayed with him while Brett and Brown tugged and hacked at such saplings as they could find and handle, managing to make a wobbly litter. It took time. After they started off again their progress, carrying Malone, who stayed unconscious, was slow. It was growing dark before they were out of the woods, Occasional rays, rapidly nearing the horizontal, showed them their direction and that they were working out of the trees toward the canyon at last. The litter was not easy to carry, Malone was heavy. They took turns at relieving each other, setting down their burden for the change.

The rest—or the uneven joggling—brought the injured stoker back to his senses at one of these halts and he promptly sat up, cursing. Brett's patience chafed through.

"Look here, Malone," he said. "We're not carrying you exactly because we love you, any more than you do us. Nor for any expected gratitude. But if we hadn't done it, my son, and left you where you played out—the pigs would have had meat for supper tonight—or the dogs a change of diet. Unless your pal Wolf had forestalled them to make an end of you. We're not looking for thanks and don't expect any, not from you.

Nevertheless you owe us something for toting you for the past hour or so and you can pay it back by common decency."

Malone glared at Brett but found no reply. He got to his feet stiffly. At that instant a wild boar trotted out and stood gazing at them, his up-curving tusks showing, his wicked little eyes gleaming redly. His snout was far longer than that of an ordinary pig, one shaggy ear was missing. His bristly shoulders were wide and powerful and he tapered off behind with a symmetry that spoke for great speed and agility. He stood there snuffing at them, making up his mind, challenging the right of way. When he turned his head a tusk showed up a foot or over in length, curving backward like a saber.

He displayed absolutely no fear. He grunted and another appeared, standing beside him. One was black and the other dirty white. The bristles on their backs commenced to rise; they lowered their heads and tossed them, beginning to champ their jaws and fleck them with foam while their tasseled tails switched ominously. To turn back was disaster. To advance seemed hazardous. Brett and Brown held their ground in the trail with their spears lowered, ready for a charge. Both boars grunted in unison and the woods suddenly echoed with a score of answers from both sides. The eyes of the two champions of vested rights literally blazed with fury as they rushed with wild fury and incredible speed to clear the trail.

There were trees available with boughs they could reach by a little speedy agility in climbing. But Malone was incapable of it. Brett rapped out an order to Tully over his shoulder: "Boost him up. We'll hold 'em."

He was conscious of Malone on Tully's shoulders, scrambling for refuge. Then the white boar was upon him, Brown taking the black in its charge. Brett's flinthead struck the boar in its shoulder, it grated against bone, glanced off along the thick tough hide and entered its flank. There it held against the hip, while the boar squealed and twisted and strove to rip him with its tusks. The spear shaft bent but did not break. Only the determined effort of the brute to reach and maim its opponent kept the unbarbed flint in place. Back of the boars the trail was close packed with other pigs, crowding like maggots, snorting and grunting. More were striving to break through the undergrowth. It was an affair of seconds before they would be javelined by the tusks. Malone was in the crotch of a tree, Tully still on the ground, trying to find place for a weapon thrust.

Brown's spear, taken back when Malone was carried, had pierced the chest of his boar and the shaft had snapped under the frenzied wrenching. His home-made war-club swung up and came down to shatter the brute's skull. It dropped and the smell of its blood seemed to send the rest frantic.

"Jump!" he yelled as he side-swiped at Brett's boar, smashing it over the one good ear and toppling it. "They're all over us."

Brett leaped, caught the bough above them and, as he had not done for many years, since his old gymnasium days, swung his legs up, in between his arms, knees across the branch that commenced to sway under his weight and that of Brown. He brought up sitting, breathless, a little uncertain how he had managed.

Brown was grinning beside him. The fighter had swung up sidewise, clasping the branch with arms and legs and wriggling into position astride. Tully was safe with Malone. Beneath them the herd of pigs was milling, rooting at their dead and wounded, gazing up vindictively at the trees, trampling a circle about them, grunting as they patrolled.

"We are in for it," said Brett. "Stuck here till they make up their minds to quit. Can you make out to hang on, Malone? It'll likely be a long siege!" Malone deigned no reply but Tully announced that their seat, masked from Brown and Brett, was comfortable. Brett started to edge along the bough toward the main trunk.

It was too pendulous for his liking and their feet were none too high above the pigs. It creaked ominously once as he inched in and Brown sagged downward, hauling up his knees and riding the bark like a jockey on a horse's withers. They both made the trip in safety and found wider, securer perches.

The light failed. Dusk deepened to night. They sat in the darkness knowing that the pigs still kept revengeful vigil by the patter of their hoofs, occasional grunts, and—once—for several minutes, a crunching noise that told of their method of disposal of their dead, a sound that was at once menace and warning. From time to time they called out to each other. Malone and Tully had found creepers on their tree and had cradled themselves into more security.

The blackness yielded slowly to dusk again. Motes and flecks of light made their way through the tangle of boughs. They began to distinguish the forms of their inexorable patrol, to see glints from vigilant, vindictive eyes. A beam of moonlight fought down and through, broken but persistent. Others followed, shifting their angles slowly as the moon rose.

Far off, as it had commenced the night before, they heard the clarion of the pack rising and falling, dying away. It came again but from the opposite direction, an echo, another pack or the first, circling on the trail. Silence again and uneasy grunting from the pigs—a consultation perhaps, if their shallow brains could hatch more than one idea.

Again—and again—louder and louder. Two packs. If they were hunting in unison—the idea occurred to the treed quartet simultaneously—they were closing in on the herd, either by direct scent or because this runway was also a hunting trail. There was little wind in the forest, the pungent scent might have scattered.

Round in their circle the pigs trotted, stopping every now and then to lift their shaggy ears and grunt, to shake their heads and lift their snouts toward the men they had trapped and were determined to reach. The dogs were silent but it was certain they were near at hand. They could see the wide nostrils of the pigs working as they snuffed. They ceased their circling, gathering in a compact mass, the sows in the center, the boars facing both ways down and up trail. They were trapped in their turn.

As at a signal, the woods reverberated with yelps and deep-throated barks. Green, lambent eyes showed before the leaping shapes came hurdling over and through the moonbeams, fangs gleaming as they dashed for the defiant swine. The boars confronted them. The issue joined in a maelstrom of action that was accompanied by a deafening uproar. Tusks shone as they slashed and ripped. The great body of one hound was fairly tossed in a somersault, landing among the sows that made short work of it, biting and devouring in fury rather than hunger.

But the pack—the packs—were organized. Certain dogs acted as holders, clamping their jaws on the ears of the harassed boars, holding on and anchoring with their weight while others sought for throats or sank their teeth into the softer hindquarters. The mantle of bristles on the tuskers' massive shoulders protected them, but at last a boar would be tripped, flung on side or back and instantly the entrails would be ripped out. It was a bloody, sickening affair to scent and sight and hearing. The dagger-like tusks tore through hide and muscle, the cruel fangs slashed and tore in the mad *melee.*

The herd broke at last, leaving their dead and the mangled carcasses of three of the dogs. Some of the hounds remained to devour the hogs, the rest, with unsated blood lust, streamed off after the squealing sows and grunting boars, now in full retreat. The feast below did not last long. The dogs who had filled their stomachs did not follow their fellows but trotted off down the trail. The four men clung to their boughs, shaken by the spectacle, unnerved. The pack had taken no notice of them.

All sounds died away. They waited until the moon lifted several degrees and then they got down to the sodden, trampled ground where the three hounds lay—what was left of them. Malone was able to move—his litter was not to be found and he professed himself restored. In silence they fearfully reached the edge of the forest and crossed open ground to the edge of the canyon close by the waterfall.

Up the ravine they heard a cry—a human note—a clan call. Walker and Bowman searching for them—cooeeing through the night. They answered and waited till they saw the pair coming anxiously up, carrying flaming torches. O'Neill was with the professor, who was much better, both of his bruises and the fever, but alarmed. A fire was burning brightly in the cave-mouth as they stumbled up the slope to find food waiting for them—food and safety and the welcome beds of fern.

CHAPTER X.
WAYS AND MEANS.

MALONE WAS TOO STIFF to move the next day. He lay prone on the ferns. The professor, rapidly convalescing, was the only one against whom he seemed to have no grudge. To continue searching for Wolf seemed to the rest of them waste of time for the present. He could fend for himself and he could easily elude pursuit in the forest. Malone's objection that they would not know what to do with him gathered weight. He would probably be only captured after a desperate fight in which some of them might well be injured unless they could surprise him.

Meanwhile he might come back to his senses, return to camp. Professor Harland held no grudge against him, considering him beside himself. The money was a small item. It was not likely he had destroyed it since he reckoned it a prize. It was a useless thing in their circumstances.

And there was much to be done. The cave was an unhealthful place and inconvenient. Brett wanted to push forward the building of a regular dwelling; the others were intent upon their experiments and inventions. The general health of the community demanded first attention. If they ran across Wolf or he interfered with them it would be different. The majority did not hold the tolerance for him that the professor displayed.

Bowman had thought out improvements on his weir. Instead of the straight line of stakes, he constructed with Brown two curving pounds, one larger than the other. The stone dam acted as a leader to the entrance to the larger pound, splitting the opening. There was a bypass into the smaller pound around an angling wall that left a five-foot ingress.

The fish, entering along the dam, either upstream or down, naturally followed the curving wall of the bigger pound, through the bypass into the smaller and finally into a shallow pocket about ten feet long and sixteen wide, with sides of netting stretched on a frame and a floor of wicker. The walls were made fish-tight by brush woven in and out of the stakes.

The professor solved the netting question. He discovered one day how to lay the twine, setting one strand on his knee and twisting the next about it with a rolling motion of his palm. So with the third ply, overlapping cleverly to preserve the strength of the continuous string. These three plies were in turn manufactured into rope, the lay being left-handed as opposed to a right-hand lay in the twine. Malone helped with the cordage while his strained tendons got in shape.

The weir was a success. It was an automatic fish-trap. After tide-turn all that had to be done was to bailout the shallow pocket with a hand net and bring back the catch. It offended Walker's sporting blood. He made himself hooks out of shell, bait and barb in one. A curving piece of shell for spoon, a carven hook of pearl, rubbed down on stone, tied to the shining concavity.

With this, trolling on a pole, he made good catches for his own pleasure and relaxation. But he was not above devising a shrimp net out of O'Neill's bark-cloth stretched on a frame attached to a pole. Shoving this scraper along the sands at low tide Walker caught many a mess of the savory hoppers.

With his cloth O'Neill had trouble that experience overcame. He experimented with various bark linings and finally turned out wide sheets of the papery stuff. Its texture was slightly scratchy to the skin at first. Needles and thread such as they could evolve did not work well with it. O'Neill tested out glue made from fish skin and bones to join seams, but it was not satisfactory. At last they compromised on using the stuff as skirts and mantles. Their skins hardened as they bronzed. The paper cloth was good fair-weather material.

Tully, with his pots, seemed to have tackled the hardest proposition. Baked in the sun they cracked, they would not glaze, they fell apart with boiling water or a stew. He managed to achieve some bricks of the clay mixed with chopped tree fiber and dried grass. These furnished a kiln built about a stone slab supported on two rocks.

Under this he piled charcoal; on top he arranged his clay productions. Tully got the same lesson out of his pottery as the others did with their tasks, that failures were steps to success. Experiments taught him to arrange his drafts so that the charcoal would furnish the right temperature, to set his pots mouth down, to sprinkle salt so that its fumes made the glaze. The first triumph came with mixing sand with his day.

His shapes were cause for laughter at first, misshapen crocks scooped out of a lump of clay, saucers clumsily modeled by hand. The professor suggested a potter's wheel turned by hand, and, after a week of fussing, Tully evolved one, got the hang of it and began to deliver what he proudly termed art-ceramics.

Walker was chef and purveyor. He spent hours making bows and arrows and trying to secure good aim and penetration. The ducks on the lake were his inspiration for this weapon making. The fiber string was too elastic, the wood for the bow insufficiently so. Walker's bows were good for amusement but not much more, to his good-natured chagrin. He tried a sling, he tried boomerangs and came to the decision, with the rest who practiced with his implements of chase and war, that, with primitive weapons, the main effectiveness lies in the skill of the handler, and that baffled them for many weeks.

Brett tackled the ax problem as the one that seemed to him most imperative to solve. Their attempts at felling trees would have been mocked at by an aged beaver with toothache in its incisors. Once down, they could split the saplings with wedges, get off the bark by soaking and setting them before a fire. But he wanted to get beams and planks, flat surfaces for frames and flooring. Brown built a wickiup for curing pork and they got all the pigs they wanted by pitfalls near wild yam patches.

But Brett wanted a house. The question of moving across the island was settled by a gradual dropping of the subject. It never came to open argument. There was a certain sentiment attaching to the place where they had first built a fire that appealed to all of them. And the selected site was a good one.

Brett turned surface geologist. He found flat stones in the stream that suggested to him ax-heads, plowshares and hoes, with a little ingenuity of fastening to shaft and pole and crooked bough. He got several prizes by diving into the pool below the waterfall. Many were fortuitously shaped. As hoes and plows and even spades they were quite satisfactory but he was not ready for agriculture and the best of his stones had an edge that hacked rather than cut and, with the harder woods he coveted, merely bruised.

He discovered one day a stone of close texture; roughly circular. He floated it to camp and painfully and tediously chipped away a hole for an axle. He sculpted the circumference to truer dimensions. He built a crude cradle and made a handle. Though they were still in the stone age— nowhere could they find trace of malleable metal, even of definite ore— he had stretched its limits. He had a grindstone. Axes and knives of shell or stone or bone could be kept sharp enough to be really tools, not aggravating substitutes.

He made fairly smooth surfaces now with his lumber by charring and then scraping, chiseling and adzing. He bored holes with his precious nails and pegged his timbers together. The house grew, wicker walls from the willows on the watershed, daubed with clay, O'Neill's finest bark cloth for windows until the time they substituted tortoise-shell.

Long grass furnished the thatch, bundled and bound to the crosspoles of the raftering. They built a fireplace and a chimney of stones mortared with pounded coral lime and sand, a hearthstone of a slab. This was for cooking and comfort on rainy days and cool nights, also for light. When it was nearly finished, they moved in, considering it a marvel of architectural design and builders' skill. It had many defects but it was habitable. They could have built it over again immediately and wonderfully improved it, but it was their own home; it was waterproof and windproof;

it was warm with a fire and cool without one. A ladder reached to it from the ground.

In the narrow crack of the cliff where the spring rose they established their larder for spare food, finding a shallow cave that they believed out of the reach of the dogs. Food spoiled rapidly at that season. Throughout the day there was a good deal of heat, though one day in three brought some rainfall, and hardly a day passed that was not partially cloudy. Every little while there would be a smart downpour and such nights would be really cold. If there was a rainy season to come they foresaw the need of warmer clothing than O'Neill's output.

To supplement the pottery they used shells and some calabash gourds discovered by Malone. He continued cranky after he was on his legs again. When he could not have the company of the professor he stayed alone, a chip always on his shoulder, holding fast to some resolution that the others looked down upon him, whereas he knew—and the professor knew—that he was as good a man as any, if not better. When Brett and O'Neill started swimming lessons after the house was built, Malone would not join the class but watched them and applied what he learned in private. Eventually he swam as well as any of them.

With the stress of early labors they did not miss amusements. There was more than enough to do and sunset saw them glad to eat their supper and turn in to be up with the dawn. But when the work began to slacken Brett saw the necessity of something to fill in. With leisure, joshing was likely to slide unperceived into wrangling. They were often at a loss for subjects of discussion. After Professor Harland finished his Aeneid and other translations of the classics stored in his memory, O'Neill came to the rescue with stories—somewhat vainglorious—of the film studios. The others opened out, little by little, but too soon all yarns became twice-told and then twenty-times stale.

The swimming helped. They devised other sports and games, making quoits out of shells, throwing at a mark, practicing with the bows and arrows. They organized trips to hunt out Wolf, but though they found traces of him here and there they never sighted him nor did he bother them. Some of these signs were the remains of raw fish and roots.

It was the sleepless hours after dark that palled. Professor Harland suggested checkers and they pyrographed a board and played with black and white flat stones for men. Tully, who had some talent in that direction, drew a map of the island on bark with a hotpoint made of a nail. Naming the various points was one pastime. Tully insisted on titling the chart as *The Isle of Nowhere* and in time it fairly bristled with more or less apt nomenclature.

In many trips Walker managed to shoot three ducks and the professor made pens from their largest quills. Walker contributed the ink bag of a small cuttle fish, only to find the fluid insoluble in water. The sediment, however, made a sort of cake and, by treating it with the lye water from wood-ashes used in their soap-making they produced ink. But they had to discard the pens. They scratched the fine bark-paper and even the bark linings and the ink blotted.

Brushes were manufactured from chewed twigs and from feather tips. The professor started on a fresh rendition of his precious Virgil and Brett kept a diary. The water-clock they contrived finally with one of Tully's cylinder jars; the sundial, with all their attempts, proved uncertain and irregular.

Out of the logs, hollowed by charring and their stone tools, they made two, dugout canoes, outrigged, furnished first with paddles, then with mast and lateen sails of matting or, for light breezes and fine weather, bark-cloth. Rain saturated the latter and they soon discarded it. Walker chose the shaping of the two canoes as his special job and displayed considerable ingenuity. He chiseled away stem and stern, he added a prow and built up gunwales of uneven planking, fastened by pegs. The little craft sailed fast on the wind but it was long before they overcame leeway and could beat to windward.

They found other edible fruits from time to time, notably that of a passion-flower vine, acidulous and refreshing. Substitutes for tobacco were hard to discover. They either lacked in flavor, burned the tongue or would not burn at all in the pipes they made of hollowed roots, with stems of rushes or pithy slender twigs with the centers pushed out.

Time dragged for most of them. It was braked by the thought of Home. The inadequacy of a substitute heightened nostalgia by comparison with the real article. After a while they ceased to mention such things, but they brooded, with the exception of Professor Harland, working at his hexameters, and Brett.

Brett reveled in the life, in every difficulty overcome. His muscles developed, he became able to work long hours without fatigue; his appetite was astounding and his digestion excellent. The physical side of him came into its own and, with it, the desire for labor and keen joy of achievement.

They started an attempt at a boat, chopping out a keel and posts for stem and stern. The ribs were a harder job and despite all their efforts they botched them. Most of the available wood was green, it warped and split. The skeleton was asymmetrical despite their best pains. It took days to hack and scrape out a plank. At last they gave it up in despair and burned the travesty. Disputes, quarrels and contradictions became more frequent while Malone, sometimes covertly, sometimes openly, sneered at Brett's endeavors to promote mutual interests and entertainment. Even Brown's good nature languished to moodiness. A day of rain brought melancholy; sunshine failed to restore normality. Walker's whistle failed; jocularity vanished; a laugh was almost a forgotten thing.

Brett had found life as he had never known it. The others had lost life as they had imagined it. Malone's influence began to assert itself. Tully and Bowman began to listen to his vulgarities. Sex instincts worked in them unhealthily. Their moral senses dulled.

They often heard the cry of the pack but lacked incentive to try to secure their hides for leather. When it was cold they hugged the fire.

Brett broached the subject of plantations of rice-fields and yam cultivation but gained no response.

"What's the use?" asked Tully. "We get along as well as one can in this —— hole."

"We can improve the quality. We don't know how the weather will act after a while. It may rain for weeks on end. We should put up stores. We ought to look to the future. We've got to face the fact that we may never get away from here."

"You seem to be reconciled to it."

"I am, Bowman. That isn't quite true. I like it."

"You needn't be so ruddy smug about it," cut in Malone. And talk languished. Brett blamed himself for the growing apathy, the breaking down of moral fibers and of civilization where he had thought to upbuild. If he really had those qualities of leadership he had fancied he felt in him,

surely he could devise some means of making the best of things, of knit-
ting them together. He did not realize the strength of his opponent—
Homesickness, fed by Memory, natural instincts and longings.

He took counsel with Professor Harland, with Walker.

"They are younger than we are," said the professor. "Tully, Bowman
and O'Neill are only boys. Brown is married. Malone has led a rough life
and he has acquired habits and appetites that are hard to down. It is only
natural they should be restive. The beacon has been a big disappointment."

The beacon had been built, not on the crater but on the cliff summit
back of the house, a narrow trail made to it so that one might rush up
with a flaming torch at the first sight of a ship. In all fine weather some
one always remembered to watch beside the beacon. Hope died hard and
left aching scars of disappointment. There were so many hours of night,
of storm and rain, when some ship might have marked the horizon!

Walker hit the nail on the head.

"Plain 'omesick. Seen it in the war. Known a man to 'urt 'imself—
not becos 'e was afraid but becos 'e wanted to go 'ome for a spell. Brown's
worrying about his missus and the kids. W'y not? I would if I 'ad 'em.
O'Neill used to be a big toad in a puddle. He misses all that. Lord, I bet
'e was fed on kisses and girl mush. Tully an' Bowman, they want girls and
dances—strolling down a shady lane with 'er 'and in mine. They can't stop
thinkin' about it. They ain't monks. Nor me either, for that.

"I'm a bit fed up on it all myself. It looks like a clean washout and I
like my bit of fun. Malone's a roughneck. Most of all 'e misses 'is booze.
'E's been tryin' to make some. Tully and Bowman 'ave sampled it. O'Neill's
got no use for Malone. Won't talk to 'im. They've tried guavas and grapefruit and yams, but there ain't enough sugar in the stuff. It ferments a bit
but it makes 'em sick. I took one swig. Enough for me. 'E's workin' on
berries now. Some day 'e'll strike the combination and there'll be ructions.
We ought to start another boat."

"We can't build a boat, Walker. Not a plank one. We'd have to steam
the planks and wooden pegs would draw. Look at the best planks we've
made. And those ribs. We've no compass."

"Those chaps are nigh ready to take a chance on a raft, Brett. You
try and figger out some sort of a boat. It'll help keep their pecker up.
Something may break before it's finished."

Brett thought hard and worked hard to design one. He knew something of sailing. He spent long hours on the lagoon with the best dugout, changing the rig. He found that by using boom and gaff, a club jib and a tiny lateen mizzen he could work to windward. He knew that South Sea islanders had made long voyages successfully in their native craft. It was surely within the scope of a white man to do the same. But those islanders had handed down lore of stars and of currents, they could take easily acquired stores of coconuts, yam paste and dried fish.

For himself he was content. So was the professor. The latter had spoken once about his daughter. "They grow away from us, our children," he said. "They make their own nest, their own lives. We become but shadows to them. She has mourned for me but she has her fill of compensations. I used to think," he went on, "that children were one's patent of immortality. I have changed my mind. It is what a man does, what he creates and hands down to posterity. It stands for itself. Nothing is wasted."

"Your Aeneid?"

"I trust so. It may survive. I have published one edition. Who knows? The children of Caesar are forgotten dust, but the songs of Omar the Tentmaker will live. What you have done here, on this island, Brett, what you will yet do, will not be wasted. Effort is power translated. It may change shape and form; it never is lost."

Brett began to see a dim possibility of a seaworthy craft. It seemed to him that most of them stood midway between the danger of decadence and the perils of the sea. Perhaps the last chance was the best. Some diversion was a vital necessity.

Then Brown came rushing in from their platform veranda. "The dogs have smelled out the hams and stuff," he cried. "There's a pack of 'em at the larder. The devils have jumped up on each other and clawed up into the cave. Come on!"

They grabbed weapons and torches and raced out. They cornered the dogs in the cleft before the brutes noticed them. A brand or two flung in maddened them. Instead of fleeing they charged in deadly earnest, singling out individuals, employing the tactics they used on the hogs.

Spear thrusts failed to stop them, clubs stunned one of two but they slashed with their teeth, trying for a grip, they scored with their claws and Tully went down with his forearm in a beast's jaws to defend his throat.

Brett and Brown leaped in, battering with club and ax.

A dog sprang for Brown's neck. The fighter's hand shot out and he gripped the brute by its own throat, swinging it clear of the ground while it clawed at him. Brett, swinging his ax, killed the one that had Tully's arm, spattering the latter with blood, then helping him to rise. He saw Brown toss aside the dead body of his hound, fairly choked, and bend to find his weapon. A slavering beast seized his leg and again Brett's weapon crushed home.

Malone was fighting with fire, dashing the flaring wood into open jaws that snapped at it but retreated. But they were all too exposed with their tender skins to risk an open fight. The thought of hydrophobia flashed through Brett's mind as he shouted to them to make for the ladder and the house.

Some one threw a torch. It caught in the drying ferns and a line of fire ran across the opening and spread suddenly. It was too much for the pack. Terror struck them, remembrance of forest fires when they had been forced to race for their lives. They turned tail and fled leaving their victors to extinguish the flames as soon as the last of the raiders disappeared. Tully had gone to the house to treat his arm, Brown with him, lame on a lacerated leg. As the others stamped out the final sparks they heard a wild laugh high above them. Looking up they saw the figure of Wolf, naked against the moonlit sky, gesticulating and dancing. Then it vanished.

In the middle of the night, with the wounds bandaged and all asleep, a great boulder came hurtling through the roof of the house, breaking thatch and floor. Another followed and another, narrowly missing them. They ran out and the bombardment ceased. The skyline was still luminous and once again they saw Wolf, bending over, yelling incoherencies down at them, bursting into maniacal laughter. Suddenly he vanished. Brett and Walker started to scale the trail.

Before they reached the summit there was a red flare in the heavens. Atop the cliff they saw the beacon burning fiercely. Wolf was nowhere to be seen. But he must have stolen fire, the idea forming in his apish brain after seeing them fight the dogs. They kept a fire burning in good weather in a big ring of stones to offset the bother of remaking. He had crept down and taken a burning bough. Wolf had gone amuck. He was bent on their destruction.

CHAPTER XI.
WOLF.

THE NEXT DAY Brett, Walker, Bowman and O'Neill started out in grim earnest to hunt Wolf down. He could not be allowed to remain at large. Brown and Tully nursed their wounds. They kept up a treatment of cold water bandages as the best at hand. The wounds seemed healthy and inclined to heal, a tribute to their open life. The professor acted as nurse and Malone remained as guard.

He had discovered a bitch lying in the cleft. She had been stunned and was in whelp. By one of the quirks in his nature Malone determined to win her friendship and bring up the pups as playmates. One of the beast's legs was cut with a spearhead, practically hamstrung and she could not get away. Malone took her water which she lapped after he was out of sight. He was confident that hunger and maternal instincts would bring her to accept hospitality. He meant to keep her until the pups were weaned. If she remained stubborn they could be tamed. He made a bed of ferns for her and placed food near her, disclaiming all thought of sympathy.

"A pup or two'll come in handy for company," was all he vouchsafed.

The hunt was without result. They kept it up for a week, scouring the island, but Wolf, dodging or hiding in trees, eluded them. Twice they saw smoke, once they ran across warm ashes. He had managed to retain his fire or, stimulated by its past possession, had managed to combine flint and stone.

Brown's leg healed first. Tully's arm still bothered him. The muscles had been lacerated and they responded slowly to treatment. The great luck they had had was lack of serious illness or accident. Professor Harland was heavier and stronger, their balanced diet agreed with them. Malone helped to repair the house while the chase for Wolf was on. The disaster seemed to have knit them all together a little. He had got to the point where he could touch the bitch. Toward the rest she maintained invincible hostility. The litter was born the day they gave up the pursuit of Wolf. Malone protested strenuously against moving her and they found a temporary larder.

They had furniture now. Tables, chairs, hammocks. The food was dished up. They had individual plates, knives and forks carved from hog bones and tusks. The bark cloth was easy to manufacture and they used it for towels. One thing Brett had insisted upon and Walker and Tully had backed him, the maintained sanitation of the camp. Garbage was burned or buried. Before they went out after Wolf they had skinned the dead dogs and they worked on the hides with water, salt, lye-water and ashes, scraping them clean, securing in the end fairly soft leather.

The matter of jerkins, breeches, shoes was only one of ingenuity and supply. Hats were plaited by the professor. In two months they had emerged from disaster to comparative comfort. Their bodies were cared for. Only their minds needed salvage.

The house was on the north side of the canyon. To the west trees grew thickly on the slope of the cliff. To the east they were scarcer. The place was shady but basked in the afternoon sun. They no longer thought about moving. They had gone a few times on a picnic to the southern harbor, visiting the hot springs and the beach, where they caught a few turtles. Yet discontent smoldered.

Brett, coming back from his boating, would find them sitting silent. The committees were broken up. The necessary work got barely done and that was all. Malone played with his puppies when the mother would let him. Professor Harland painted his hexameters. Walker tried his hand at making a fiddle and failed. Tully and Bowman had made a set of dominos but lost taste for the game. Time dragged and dragged.

There came two days of fierce storm; the river in spate, furious winds, trees crashing. Then a week of strong sunshine, with a spell of humidity that sapped their energies. The ferns crisped, grasses yellowed, leaves fell from the trees. Stones were blistering to the touch, the island seemed desiccating. They lost their appetites and with them tempers. Brett strove for control against the gibes of Malone who lost no opportunity for jeering on every occasion. At the end of the fourth week the bitch disappeared. She had lost her milk and interest in her litter. They were practically weaned but four of the seven died and Malone soured more than ever.

"What he needs is a good licking," said Brown. "I'd like to give it to him but he leaves me alone."

"No sense in starting anything."

"It 'ud do 'im a lot of good. Why don't you give it to 'im when he sneers at you?"

Brett stared. He knew he was not a coward but he had always figured that a personal clash with the husky oiler would mean his own defeat. He had no desire to display his own inferiority or lose prestige. That was natural enough.

"Yes, you," Brown went on. "You're built right. Look at the muscle you've put on. You're solid as I am. You've got the devil's own reach. I don't suppose you've been in a scrap all your life, but if you 'ad a little science I'd pick you for a nasty one to tackle. You ain't the same man who came off the steamer."

It was true enough, though Brett had scarcely realized the extent of his development. He knew he could lift weights easily that once he would never have dreamed of attempting. He could paddle with any of them, haul, fell trees.

"If I 'ad your noodle I'd be champion," persisted Brown. "Though a lot of good it would do me. What say we spar a bit—for the fun of it?"

Brett hailed this as a welcome exercise. Brown went with him in the canoe and they would land and box—open-handed at first, then with their fists padded in bark-cloth. Brown got to calling him Fitzsimmons, only half in jest, for Brett developed a good judgment of distance, effective footwork and a capacity for landing staggering blows.

"I'd give 'alf my meals for a week to see you tackle Malone," he said one day. "You'd give 'im the shock of 'is life." But Brett saw no wisdom in open quarreling.

Wolf struck for the second time with a maniac's craft and malice. Once more he chose the middle of the night. The rain had held off, the season seemed changing, the woods were dry as tinder. They had been careful of their fires. And they had forgotten the burning of the beacon, since replaced.

They woke to the fierce roar of a conflagration that gathered way and force with astounding speed. Wolf had set fire to the timber on the east and the draft that always sucked up the canyon at nightfall had fanned it swiftly beyond control. Tongues of flame leaped up, blazing fragments rocketed ahead of the main fire, carried up in the heated air, dropping down to start fresh flares.

Crackling, snapping, seething, with explosions that sent live masses leaping up in volcanic blasts, the flames swept on. The house was doomed by the time they were down the ladder. The tremendous heat drove them down to the river, across it, where they watched the total destruction of all their labor. The camp was obliterated in a moment, devoured in the maw of the moving furnace. They saved practically nothing. Malone dragged out his whining puppies. The professor snatched his precious sheets and Brett saved his diary. That was all. Home, its belongings, clothes, labor, everything was wiped out, except the canoes and the weir. Even they were scorched.

They stood on the farther bank, realizing the extent of their disaster.

"I'd like to catch 'im and chuck 'im in the middle of it," said Walker at last. " 'Is island, 'e told Malone. So 'e tried to burn us alive."

"It might have been accidental," said Brett. "A chafing bough would have done it this weather."

The contradiction came pat to his sentences. Wolf stood on the cliff at the top of the waterfall, his body copper-bright in the glow of the fire, sweeping on up the canyon. He cupped his hands and shouted something they could not hear and jumped up and down in devilish glee or in rage that they had escaped. They had no weapons, so soundly had they slept and so little time had been given them. They started for him empty-handed, Malone thrusting his puppies into the arms of the professor.

He was out of sight when they gained the head of the fall. The rocks held no tracks; the glare of the fire revealed nothing. But they kept on, naked as they were, for they had been sleeping through the heat without even covering. They divided, splitting up into groups that broke again, seeking for a chance to give the view-halloo. Brett found himself with Malone, racing along the cliffs toward the watershed. Tully and Bowman made toward the woods. Walker and O'Neill headed at a tangent for the swamp. Brown kept to the bed of the ravine.

The thinning woods slowed the fire on the other side. The main forest would not be touched. The swamp would check it to the south if it turned that way. It would probably die out on the short turf and willows of the saddle. A pall of smoke rolled up, the westering moon shining on it. The canyon floor and the cliffs were bright with a ruddy glare.

As they neared the junction of the tributary flowing south with the main river, Brett caught sight of Brown running fast and with apparent purpose. He looked up, caught sight of them and shouted, pointing ahead.

Malone gave a cry. "There he goes!"

Wolf was well away, close to the source of the river. In a few minutes he reached the slope that ran sharply down to the west, ending in a wide crevasse that might have been made by earthquake. Its deep bottom was thick with trees but its almost vertical sides were bare. They had searched it twice for Wolf after finding the remains of a fire in the glen.

Brown was much closer to Wolf than Brett and Malone. The going was better for him and the crossing of the tributary had delayed them. But they panted on, getting their second wind, resolute for punishment. They topped the last rise and saw Brown closing in on Wolf with a tremendous burst of speed, striding down the declivity at a headlong pace that seemed almost certain to plunge him into the gulf. Wolf angled off, glancing back.

He saw Brett and Malone heading him away from the only practical descent into the glen, hesitated, ran on, then turned at bay on the edge. He had his club with him and swung it as Brown, checking himself with difficulty but carrying speed, ran in on him.

The club came down. It looked as if it had landed on Brown's head but the crafty fighter ducked, side-stepped, caught the uplifting arm as it whirled for a second blow. He smashed a blow at Wolf's stomach and caught him higher—over the heart. The madman staggered from the impact, but the punch did not seem to hurt him. Brown followed up, smashing for the jaw. The slug went home to the point and Wolf's head rocked, yet he seemed insensitive of the jar save as the success of the blow infuriated him. He wrenched free from Brown's grip and swung his dub again. It struck Brown's shoulder and he sagged. Brett groaned as he strove to mend his pace. He had outstripped Malone but he was still two hundred yards away.

Brown clinched and the two figures, locked together, swayed on the very verge. Once Wolf fairly lifted the prizefighter from his feet and whirled him toward the abyss. Somehow Brown entangled his legs and the two fell, rolling, striking. Brett pounded on. The twisting pair writhed closer and closer, Wolf on top, raining down blows with his fists. He had lost his club in the wrestle and one of them had kicked it over the edge.

Brown heaved. Brett saw his knees go up. Wolf toppled and Brown got on his hands and knees, facing the gulf. Brett was twenty yards away.

Wolf leaped on the back of his opponent, striving to throttle him. Up shot Brown's hands, clamping the other's wrists. Brett was close enough to see the muscles bunching on the fighter's back as he made his final effort. Wolf parabolaed through the air, half hauled, half propelled, over Brown's head and went whistling down into the deep rift. As Brett arrived on the edge the man's body struck the slope, somersaulted, struck again and went rolling, rolling down to the tree tops far below. Brown flopped over on his back exhausted.

"It was 'im or me," he gasped. "Broke my shoulder, I think. Busted my ribs. Fought like a—go-rill—" He straightened out with limbs twitching, unconscious.

"Some scrap," grunted Malone, kneeling with Brett beside the senseless winner. "He had better luck than I did. We're through with Wolf."

They were. They made their way down the glen later but they found only what the wild pigs had left of the Slovak.

CHAPTER XII.
REACTION.

IN THE TORRID WEATHER that prevailed for two weeks after the disaster they lived from hand to mouth. All Brett could finally prevail on them to do was to erect a grass shelter not far from the hot springs. They fished and grubbed enough to live upon, fortunate in finding turtles' eggs. They seemed stunned by the loss of all they had labored for. And the heat sapped their energies. The professor began to wilt again. Brown's injuries bothered him and Brett feared their surgery was insufficient. His shoulder blade seemed splintered; two ribs were undoubtedly crushed.

Walker and O'Neill passed their days on the beach, gazing gloomily out to sea. Walker's slogan of "are we down'earted" changed to a sullen challenge of "w'ot's the blooming use?" Malone, with his puppies, consorted with Tully and Bowman. The canoes remained where they were in the river beside the neglected weir. Brett himself felt the languor of the enervating warmth and wondered how long it would last. Gradually his ambition returned.

Much of his time was put in looking after Brown and coaxing the professor to eat. He looked at the others with their shaggy beards, their rags of clothing, unwashed bodies; their broken, dirty nails, their dejected mien—and reacted to it.

"We are acting like a bunch of quitters," he said to Brown. "I've discovered one thing, the line between man and brute is a fine one. A comb and a cake of soap go a long way toward civilization. We can do everything over again better and quicker than we did before. Let's hop to it."

"You can't do anything with 'em," said Brown. "They've lost 'eart. They've made up their minds they've got to live 'ere till they croak and they don't care 'ow they do it."

"Well, I do. And I'm going to reorganize."

"More power to you," said Brown. "Wish I could 'elp you more."

Brett called a council at the evening meal but got little response. A call for committees on the original plan met with a laugh from Malone.

"Wolf thought he owned the island," he jeered. "If you think, you do—you don't. I'm enjoying myself. So are the boys. To —— with your system!"

Brett looked at him closely. He remembered Walker's remark about the liquor and wondered if Malone had been able to make some. They had found a species of sorghum that they chewed like sugar cane. Crushed, the juice might ferment. The three had been going off down the beach of late and staying all day. He had seen the smoke of a fire and Tully's hands had been daubed with clay more than once as if he had resumed his pottery, though he had displayed no results.

That night rain fell. Brett lay out in it for a while after he awakened. It was warm but the air was cooling fast. It rained the next day and the next and then it cleared but continued cloudy. The hot spell had passed. There was a manifest revival of spirits but no disposition to get together again. Brett persuaded Walker to go with him for one of the canoes. They took the professor back on the trip for the next one.

"I've got an idea," he confided to them as they sailed outside the reef. "I've been working it out for a long time. If the chaps will pitch in and rebuild, put us where we were before, I'll give them the means of getting away. I can make a seaworthy craft. It won't be pretty and it won't make a record for speed, but it will be fairly safe. It really isn't my own idea. It came out of stories I have read, piecing the details together, thinking it out a bit and experimenting a little—before we were burned out.

"It will be a hazardous trip, but they are going to the dogs here and if they want to tackle it I believe there's a fair chance of their making the South American continent before their food gives out. The main winds are northeast and southeast. They might be more favorable for my type of boat. It may mean landing in Chili or up nearer Panama. Their best chance of all will be to be picked up by some freighter or vessel plying from the Panama Canal to Australia. It's a gamble."

"How long will it take to build?" asked Walker.

"I should say ten weeks—say three months—with all hands putting in half time."

"Why half time? W'ots the sense in making a lot of pottery and furniture and stuff we can't take with us? Or building a big 'ouse?" Walker was plainly interested in the plan. He sat up, his wrinkled face in its frame of ginger whiskers shining with eagerness. He seemed ten years younger.

"Because I don't intend to have to do it all myself after the boat leaves."

"You're not going?" The steward's face was a study of astonishment.

"No. I like this place. I am going to make something of it. I am healthier and stronger, happier—or *as* happy—than I have ever been. This island of Nowhere can be made a garden in time."

"An Eveless Eden. Not for mine."

"We'll get along without Eves. There are no serpents anyway. I'm going to stay. Anyone else is welcome to go or leave. And I'm not going to live like a savage. We've shown what can be done as a start. Lord, man, it's like opening a mine and leaving it. Back home I was a go-between, a middleman of adventure, a dealer in other men's stories. I don't know how many of those writers lived the sort of thing they described. I'm going to.

"Maybe I'll write a book about it. If you chaps get clear, you can send me down some supplies. I've some property over there that can be realized upon—a few thousand dollars—so I won't miss what Wolf stole. I suppose that's gone. If I can get seeds down here, some tools, a book or two, I'll make a Paradise out of this. And I'll be my own man."

"You'll be that all right. You know what the French say. Everyone to 'is taste. I'll tyke my chance on the boat. 'Ow about you, prof?"

Harland smiled at Brett amiably. He was getting back his strength again. His face was flushed with the sea wind and his eyes were bright.

"If you men would send me some pen and ink and a few books, including my last edition of the Aeneid, published by The Cosmos Company of Boston, when you make Brett's shipment, I am inclined to think I shall stay with him. It will be a wonderful opportunity to rewrite my work."

"—— b'li'my!" ejaculated Walker. "Who'll ever see it?"

"This place will be on the map some day, Walker. And I fancy it will be worth while putting there. I don't think Brett wants to—to hog it. Just to make something of it. I can understand his feelings."

Walker scratched his head.

"I'm blowed if I can," he said. "Tell us about the boat."

"I'll have a model in a day or two. Then we'll talk."

Brett's plan was a big catamaran, to be formed of two of the largest logs they could find. These would be double outriggered to port of one canoe and starboard of the other. They would build up gunwales and, if possible, provide for water-tight compartments for extra buoyancy and to avoid superfluous bailing. They would be made with thwarts for paddling.

Across them, amidships, he intended to build a stout platform. The masts, main and jigger, would go through the floor and be stepped and braced on other connecting timbers. The deck would give head-room for paddlers when the wind failed. There would be a deck-house sturdy enough to resist the weather, thatched and with sides of interwoven boughs.

He had to combine lightness with strength. The sails would be their closest matting and extra ones would be carried with the stores. Water would have to be stowed in jars. They could winnow rice, smoke hams, dry fish, take a certain amount of fresh vegetables and fruit. Navigation would be due east with allowance for the winds. If the southeast wind prevailed they would pick up the north star before long.

He made his working model with the two canoes, working in an inlet, Walker aiding him and the professor. Brown he took into the secret. The others did not disturb him. He had to take the craft into the open to demonstrate his sail plan, but it seemed to arouse no excitement ashore.

They beached the *Hope*, as the model was called, in anticipation of the larger craft, at sunset, and Brett broached his project after the meal.

"There's the model," he said. "I should call it a success. It's up to you to say whether you want to take the chance."

Silence held for a minute while their faces grew sanguine. Malone spoke first, with a string of oaths. This time there was no doubt but what he had been drinking some sort of alcohol. Tully and Bowman did not show it so plainly. In the flush of his experiment Brett had not noticed them particularly.

"Going to stay behind, are you?" said Malone. "That suits me to a T. Maybe we'll manage to get along without you. But it you think we're going to sweat to fix you up all snug before we go, you're crazier than Wolf. I'm going to tell you what I think of you, you ——"

Brett stopped the flow of oaths with a straight punch to the mouth. He knew as he stepped back that he had been aching to give Malone a beating for weeks. There was no better time than this—if he would fight.

Malone wiped away the blood with a dash of his hand.

"I'll make a pulp of you!" he said.

The rest tried to interfere, but Brown called them off.

"You leave him alone," he said. "This is going to be good. If it lasts long enough."

It was a vicious enough encounter. Malone rushed, swinging with both fists, clutching at Brett when he countered with hard jolts to the face and side. He fought foul, punching for the groin, using his knees, but Brett was cool and broke the clinch undamaged, ending it with an uppercut that staggered Malone and broke his confidence.

Malone's head seemed to clear as he fought. And he was a master of rough and tumble work. Brown danced about the pair calling to Brett not to mix it. There was no question of seconds or of regular rounds. It was a test of skill and endurance.

Once Brett slipped, dropped to one knee and Malone started to kick him in the ribs. Brown darted in and flung him back.

"You fight fair!" he said. "Or I'll lick you myself!"

Brett's muscles were recently developed and his coordination sharpened by the trials of island living. Malone had the heavier slogging power, the shoulder equipment of the coal-heaver. When he got home a blow it fell like a sledge-hammer. Brett felt his strength being pounded out of him. His arms grew heavy; his fists seemed lumps of lead. Malone had closed one of his eyes, his lungs labored and he could taste the blood that overcharged the membranes of his mouth.

He feinted and tapped Malone lightly on the jaw. The oiler lunged for him, broke through his guard and hammered him on the side of the neck and back of one ear. He felt himself growing dizzy, his knees failing him; he saw Malone through a mist. He had only a few tricks after all. He had shot his bolt. He grappled with Malone, leaning on him, trying to control the other's flailing arms, sinking his face on Malone's shoulder.

"'Old 'im! 'Old 'im!" Brown's voice, far away.

A thump landed on his kidneys, stabbing him with pain. Malone had the heel of one hand under his chin, forcing it back. Dully Brett struggled to avoid the blow. A spurt of energy came to him and he brought up his left, blindly enough. It caught Malone full in the nose and the blood gushed out. Brett felt his grasp loosening and stepped back, though he thought he would fall. Friendly hands caught him and he found himself sitting on the knee of Walker. Some one dashed water in his face, gave him some to drink.

The haze cleared and he saw Malone sitting on a rock, arms dangling, the blood pouring from his nose. Brown appeared from seemingly thin air.

"Got 'im going," he said. "Stand off and fight 'im next time. 'E's got more than 'e's sent." Brett grasped the idea that the pause was one of mutual consent. Malone had stepped back when he did. No one was attending the oiler.

"Go and give him some water," he said to Walker.

"You save your breath. 'Ere, Tully, chuck some over 'im."

"Time."

Malone was more cautious until he found Brett commencing to outrange him. Brett discovered he could reach the other's face almost at will with his left. And he knew he was going to win the fight. He met a wild rush with a hard jab and, as Malone stood head to head with him and began to swing, he mixed it. He could hear the excited yelling of the little ring and Walker's reiteration:

"Upstairs. Oh, 'it 'im upstairs!"

The meaning of this came to him in a flash. He jolted his right up from the hip. It traveled less than a foot and struck against bone. Some thing cracked in his hand. But Malone slumped, sagging to the ground and Brown stood over him counting exultantly.

"No rules in this fight," said Walker, "but 'e may as well count 'im out. You copped 'im a sweet one."

Malone raised his head at nine but dropped it again. It was Brett who helped him to rise. To his astonishment, Malone, swaying groggily, grinned at him with his bloody mouth and the grin was friendly. More, he extended his hand.

"You win," he said. "I didn't think you could do it, but you're the better man. I'm licked. And I'm back of you after this." He spat out a tooth and wiped his gory face. "I mean it, Brett. You're *there*. I know when I'm licked. That ends it. Put it there."

It was fifteen weeks instead of Brett's estimated twelve, when the *Hope* stood out to sea through the entrance of the southern harbor. The model catamaran escorted her, running almost out of sight of land, reluctant to leave the argonauts. The larger boat sailed well, but the lesser kept close until the breeze strengthened, well off shore. A sweep was rigged as rudder and Walker was the helmsman. The others clustered by him.

"*Oh rewar,*" he shouted. "If we get through, you'll see me back again."

"Good luck to you!"

Brett lowered his sail and came about. His eyes were dim. As they beat up for the island he watched the *Hope* diminishing until only her big sail showed golden in the sun. Then he turned to his companions. There were two of them. Malone, at the last minute, had elected to stay.

"Out there I don't amount to much," he said. "Plain mucker, that's me. I'd be it again before long. So I'm going to stick with the prof and you, Brett. I wouldn't wonder but what I'll make quite a farmer, after all. I'd hate to leave my pups, an' I'd hate to see 'em seasick. I guess I'll stay— if I'm welcome?"

One other thing Malone had done. When the lists were being made out—letters written, arrangements planned to send or bring back supplies to the island, Malone handed Brett the money taken from the professor.

"I had a hunch where Wolf put it," he said. "I twigged it when we went down into the glen and found what was left of him. There was a hollow in a tree and a bit of bark was knocked off. At the time the money wouldn't do me any good and I wasn't aimin' you should get it. I haven't any kale of my own, but, if you want to tip me a reward, for — sake ask 'em to send me a pound or two of real smoking tobacco, will you?"

The three—Brett, Harland, Malone—climbed the peak on the eastern promontory and caught a last glimpse of the *Hope*. Below them, on the beach margin, half hidden by shade trees, stood their bungalow. The triangle of sail, only a speck on the horizon, burnished by the sun, dwindled—vanished. They looked at each other with the unasked question in their eyes. Then they went slowly down the crater.

THE END

Made in United States
Orlando, FL
08 May 2022

17638645R00095